Best Wishes

Harold H Henderson

Harold H. Henderson

QUEEN OF SPADES

THE PERMANENT PRESS
RD 2 Noyac Road, Sag Harbor, N.Y. 11963

THE PERMANENT PRESS
RD 2 Noyac Road, Sag Harbor, N.Y. 11963

QUEEN OF SPADES

Harold H. Henderson

1.

It had started raining, light but steady, as it had been threatening to do all day. Dusk, as a result of the thick clouds, had settled in early and visibility was rapidly diminishing. She could barely see the store front in the small shopping center where her car was parked in the first row. The rain beat a steady, irritating tattoo on the roof of the car, which only added to her impatience.

"Why doesn't he hurry," she thought as she sat in the car waiting. She was extremely uncomfortable and nervous. This part of the city was alien and unfamiliar to her; she had avoided it most of her adult life. Rick, her son, realized this and she couldn't understand why he had decided to come this way. Today of all days when she was in a hurry. The shopping center was obviously old; one could tell by the shoddy store fronts, the potholed parking lot, and the seedy looking people scurrying to and from the little shops. It was, she realized, one of the poorer sections of the city and the slums crowding the tiny shopping center only increased her anxiety.

They had been on their way home when Rick had suddenly announced he needed cigarettes and had abruptly pulled from the expressway onto a side street in search of a drug store or some other place to get some. She immediately protested but he had paid her no heed. It was as if he derived a perverse pleasure in making her uncomfortable. She didn't seem to be able to communicate with him anymore. He had always been such a good boy. An only child, he had given Jason and her such pleasure when he had been growing up. Her whole life had centered around him and her husband. Maybe Jason had been right; perhaps she had mothered and tried to control him too much.

She had doted on him until he finished high school, much to his embarrassment. They had hoped he would enter the university after high school. She had planned carefully; he would study law or medicine. She could see him a successful professional man, everyone coming to him for help and advice.

In those days they had been such a close-knit, loving family. The world, for her and Jason, seemed perfect.

She was a petite brunette with a quick smile and flashing green eyes. Now in her early forties she hadn't changed all that much—not outwardly anyway—and she still caused a head or two to turn when walking down the street. Jason had been the perfect husband and, from his actions and words, she had been everything he wanted.

It was only after they had learned she would not be able to have more children that she had started feeling insecure. There were some very hard times as Jason and she had worked out this problem together. It seemed only natural that she look upon Rick as her main interest in life. Jason understood her desire to protect Rick, but within reason.

Jason saw to it that he, too, had some input in the young man's development. He made sure the boy had received a good education, participated in sports, and had an all around normal-as-possible youth. Aware of Mary's plans for Rick's future, Jason agreed and partly assisted her in

4

meeting the goals she had set for their son, for their marriage was one that had been firmly established in love and mutual respect for each other.

The Army had changed their plans. He had left a boy and returned three years later almost a complete stranger, a man. He hadn't waited for the draft but had enlisted. It had been a blow to her although Jason had taken it in stride. After Rick left she had spent several months under psychiatric care. The sessions had helped her a little but her adjustment to the situation had never been complete. The doctor had warned Jason that the fixation she had on her son was unhealthy. While she was an apparently normal and a loving wife in all other aspects of her life, he feared what damage would ensue if anything ever happened to their son.

Rick had chosen his own course. He had been to Vietnam and then Germany; a world traveler. He had changed. Self-reliant, confident, he seldom asked or heeded their advice since his return. This compounded Mary's misery. She had withdrawn more and more as she felt life passing her. She was still fairly young, "still a handsome woman," Jason told her often enough, and their relationship was as strong as ever. She had her little world of home, husband, son, and close friends. She had always been protected and loved by Jason and in turn had tried to be protective of Rick—maybe too much. The world was changing and she wasn't adapting too well. Still, she had Jason and they loved one another. It would have to be enough.

*   *   *

They were standing around the rear of the tiny tobacco shop. The room was filled with the smoke of a dozen cigarettes and cigars plus the animal smell of sweat. They had been counting money and receipts. This always seemed to increase the tension and excitement, handling large sums of money, and "Fat Charlie," the proprieter, always seemed to sweat profusely. You could see the damp armpits of his shirt and the gleam of sweat on his florid face. It turned

Barker's stomach, but he watched impassively as they completed the count and bagged the money. Then the bag man left with his bodyguard.

He had planned carefully. Months had now passed and no one had said anything out of the ordinary to him. They suspected nothing. As the weeks had passed his confidence had increased. He had been a collector for a long time. He had carefully checked receipts of winners of payoffs for months before he put his plan into action. It had been simple. Never get greedy—a couple of hundred here, a couple there. He had watched and waited. On those weeks when payoffs were low he had added a winner, never exceeding the average. The first couple of times he was so scared he thought he would collapse, but no one had noticed. He had the perfect rip-off, stealing from the stealers.

Cliff Barker, the perfect example of a petty hood. Medium height and slender build, darkly handsome. He was about thirty years old and still in reasonably good health, at least that's what the ladies told him. He was about 6 feet tall and 160 pounds. He had dark, moderately wavy hair and dark brown eyes. His skin had a definite hue that gave evidence that somewhere in his past there had been a Latin in his ancestry. A kid of the streets, he had grown up worldly-wise and tough; a completely amoral person. He owed no allegiance to anyone but himself and whoever paid the most for his services.

Tonight he was to be the last to leave the front door of the tobacco shop. Some of the people had already left through the rear door and a couple through the front of the shop. This was to divert attention and try to confuse anyone who might be watching the unusual Friday night activity at "Fat Charlie's."

It was his turn to leave. He took a final drag on his cigarette and mashed it out on the floor. He knew it irritated Charlie and that was why he did it so deliberately every Friday. He exhaled in Charlie's direction, said "So long, Fat Man," and headed for the front of the store.

Charlie just watched, with hooded eyes, saying nothing. The hate emanated from his every fiber as he watched Barker's retreating back. He didn't know what was up, only that Barker had not been told of the shift in next week's meeting place.

*   *   *

The soldiers sat impassively, waiting in the old beat-up sedan. There were three of them, two in the front seat and one in the back. They had been sitting in the parked car for thirty or forty minutes, smoking, talking, completely at ease. They were good at the waiting game. It wasn't the first time nor was it likely to be the last. It was a living. Joe Peroni, the driver, was a family man who had a part time insurance job to cover his source of income. Mike Gallagher, who sat beside Joe, was a used car salesman. The third, Tony Callucci, was an undertaker's assistant. They all had one thing in common—they were professionals. The only reason Peroni was along tonight was that he recognized Barker on sight. He had only met him once or twice but he was sure he would remember him. The other two had only seen a polaroid picture but they were also sure they would recognize him.

The darkness and rain was reducing visibility but the stores were turning on their lights and should provide enough illumination for the job. It might even make pursuit more hazardous. It would definitely reduce the number of reliable witnesses. Because of the rain everyone was staying inside or running from car to store and back, their powers of observation reduced in their single-minded purpose to stay as dry as possible. The number of people under the arcade had been reduced considerably as most of the shops were closing for the day.

Peroni suddenly broke off the conversation and sat at attention. The first collection man had just come out of the tobacco shop. There were a couple of people walking near the store fronts to keep out of the rain. He started the engine and let it idle. The other two quickly and efficiently

7

completed their preparations. The windows started fogging up and Joe started the defroster and wipers. They counted three men leaving the store front, maybe a minute or two apart. He'd be the next one. Joe put the car in drive and slowly pulled from his parking place.

*   *   *

Rick had completed his browsing and finally purchased a pack of Camel Lights. He had noticed the unusual traffic from the rear of the store but thought nothing of it. A man came from the back and stopped to buy some cigarettes. Rick noticed there was a slight resemblance, more in size and weight than anything definite, and he was wearing a dark suit. Rick turned and walked out the door.

His mother would be waiting and he knew it would five or ten minutes of haranguing before she got off the smoking bit and why did he have to stop here. He didn't mean to be that way but there was something that had happened to him along the way that had left a perverse streak in him. He paused outside the shop to get his bearings and prepare to light up. Out of the corner of his eye he caught the movement of the car approaching from his left and realized he'd have to wait until it passed before he dashed to his car which he had finally spotted a few yards down to his right in the first row. He turned to his right to stay under the arcade until he'd be directly across from his car.

*   *   *

Just moments before Rick left the store, Mary, finally giving in to her impatience, opened the car door and rapidly exited, slamming the door behind her. The rain, though not a downpour, was enough to add to her irritation. She quickly walked across the driveway and took shelter beneath the covered walkway. That she had gotten wet during her walk only heightened her displeasure. She would give him a piece of her mind. She started up the arcade toward the tobacco shop when she realized he had come out and was standing a few feet away from her lighting a cigarette.

*   *   *

8

"It's him," said Joe as he increased speed slightly. The two passengers had rolled down their windows and each had a shotgun protruding from the open window. As they pulled abreast of the man on the sidewalk, Tony shouted, "Now." Both guns roared simultaneously, both men discharging their barrels. Rick Knorr never knew what hit him.

*   *   *

She had seen it all; the movement of the sedan, the guns protruding from the windows, then the roaring, searing blast. She saw her son's head hurl through the air like a red, ink-stained, cotton ball and slam against the brick store front, and his left arm, torn from the socket, crash through the front window with a loud explosion, showering glass inside the store. What was left of Rick Knorr was tossed against the front of the building like a heap of bloody rags.

In those moments before the blast, she had instantly perceived the danger and, driven by primeval instinct to protect her offspring, she hurled herself toward the car, with her arms upraised, as if she could stop what was happening. The driver gave a small jerk to the wheel and struck the screaming woman with his right front fender. He didn't look back and in seconds he was out of the parking lot and swallowed up in the night.

*   *   *

Inside, standing at the counter paying for his cigarettes, Barker heard the blast and he and the counter man were falling to the floor before the first glass shards had clattered and shattered on the floor. He was completely paralyzed, his mind racing frantically, but nothing could make his arms or legs move in the first few seconds. Petrified with fear, his animal cunning told him he had been the intended target. So they had known all along. With this realization came the urgency to move. He had to get out of town fast, he had to disappear—but where?

He looked wildly about him; the firing had ceased and the sudden quiet was even more terrifying. He had to force himself to react. He had to move. He jumped to his feet and

9

ran through the door and across the driveway to his parked car. He roared from the parking area and headed south, not really knowing where he was going. He had to get somewhere to stop and think. He had to have a safe haven, but he had no real friends to turn to, and he definitely couldn't go home. They'd realize their mistake within minutes or hours and be after him with a vengeance. As he drove he tried to figure out how they had discovered his theft. He'd been so careful. He also thought of the sorry state of his finances. He had about four or five hundred bucks and the clothes on his back, plus the car. The car, of course, would be a white elephant unless he could unload it fast. He had to disappear into the woodwork of life. The arm of the Organization was long and relentless; the very thought made him shudder involuntarily. If only he could return home and get his stash everything would be okay.

He didn't dare risk it; it would have to wait until later. He knew for the time being it was safe where it was and he had to look to his own safety first.

It was natural for him not to waste one thought on the two victims back in the parking lot. If he had he would only have shrugged his shoulders and said "tough titty." He finally came to the main highway heading out of town and poured on the coal. He wanted distance and he wanted it fast.

2.

Within seconds people had come running from the other nearby shops. Someone had called the police and the sirens could be heard approaching from a distance. The man from the shoe store next door took one look, turned white and stumbled over to the curb to retch. Several more curiousity seekers crowded in for a look, immediately turned away and wandered from the scene. No one at first even noticed the woman lying quietly on the sidewalk a few feet away.

The first patrol car pulled into the lot. One policeman took a look and called for detectives. The other policeman started crowd control and the preliminary search for witnesses. An ambulance came and took the woman to the hospital. As a result of the homicide, a second ambulance had to wait for permission to clear the remains. Detective Lieutenant Donelly arrived with his partner, Sergeant Vince Monero.

Donelly was 6 feet tall and stocky of build. He had sandy hair which was speckled with gray and was thinning too fast for his liking. His deep blue eyes were continually darting, probing, missing nothing. For his size he moved quickly, with a boxer's agility, which, in fact, he had been in his youth.

Sergeant Monero was the perfect counterpoise for him. About 5 feet 10 inches, slender but muscular, he was ten years younger than Donelly. He had dark curly hair and brown eyes that looked like agates when he was upset but could be soft and appealing at other times. He was a professional cop and his partner and mentor had taught him well. They worked hand-in-glove as a team. It seemed they got all the hard ones, which was a matter of pride with them, for they were good and everyone knew it.

With their arrival on the scene they went immediately to work. One of the patrolman approached and handed Donelly a billfold from the victim's body. He told the patrolman to get the medical examiner and the special homicide squad to the scene. It was going to be a long night. As he searched through the wallet Sergeant Monero returned. "No one saw anything," he said. "This will be a tough one. Everyone was inside because of the rain."

Donelly looked at him and said: "Vince, someone always sees something. There was a new pack of cigarettes by the body. Check the tobacco shop and get names. The place is on the list."

"Roger, that. Know who he is?"

"Looks like a Rick Knorr but we'll have to wait for positive ID from the lab boys. They did a good job on his face."

"I don't know what it's worth but one witness did say he thought he heard a second car, but because they were all inside, he couldn't be definite."

Donelly thought for a second and replied, "Keep checking on that, maybe someone else heard or saw it too. It could be important. This looks like a pro hit, especially because of the location."

The Medical Examiner had completed his work. "Looks like two shotguns at fairly close range. Death was immediate. Do you know who he is?"

"Not yet, just tentative."

"I'll give you a complete report in the morning. Can they remove the remains?"

"If the photographer's finished I see no reason why not." With that he lit another cigarette and sat wearily in the squad car. Why did he get the impossible ones? It was obviously a pro hit and that meant it would be a tough nut.

Sergeant Monero walked up to the car. "I talked with the counterman in the tobacco shop. The guy came in, looked around, bought a pack of cigarettes and left. The shooting happened within a second or two of the guy leaving the shop. My instincts say he's lying or at least not telling everything he knows. There was a new pack of Newports laying on the floor that had just been opened."

12

Donelly let that sink in. So there had been more than one customer in the store. Maybe the second car? "Stay with that, Vince, there may well have been a witness."

The Medical Examiner, ambulance and lab crew had finished and departed. The crowd had pretty well dissolved and the area was quiet again. Donelly sat thinking about what he knew, or more aptly, what he didn't know. The victim, if he was who the identification said he was, what was he doing here? His address indicated he lived on the other end of town in the upper middle class area. The tobacco shop had been added to the list for general surveillance as a suspected drop location. So far there was no indication there had been anything other than normal activity in the shop or surrounding area. Had there been another customer in the shop? He would probably never know for sure. The clerk would certainly never tell if there had been. He decided to return to headquarters. They could check with the organized crime task force and maybe get a lead on the killer's Modus Operandi. With a sigh he told Monero to head for the office.

He wondered about the unidentified woman. The ambulance attendant had said he didn't think she'd make it. A search of the area had turned up no purse or billfold so she would be another problem. An innocent victim. Maybe her family would report her missing and then they'd find out who she was. Right now she was "Jane Doe." He shuddered a little. That stone sidewalk had not done her face and head any good at all.

3.

He had waited about as long as he thought reasonable. Jason Knorr, 45 years old, solid of athletic build, did not run to panic. A successful salesman, he provided well for his family. He was the average upper income family man. A drink now and then after work, a couple of games of handball for the old stomach and muscle tone; he felt great. Tonight, however, he had been growing increasingly concerned. He looked at the clock again. It was after ten. Mary and Rick should have been home hours ago. He had been working in his little shop in the basement, oblivious of passing time until his stomach had told him he was hungry. It was then he became acutely aware of how late it was. This was not like Mary to stay out without calling. Rick, he wasn't too sure of anymore. The boy had really become independent since his service time, reminding him of himself at that age. But at least Rick had returned to college and was doing fairly well.

Rick and Mary. Mary and Rick. He reflected upon the strained relationship that had developed between them. But he was certain it would resolve itself. Rick's joining the Army seemed a necessary evil for while it destroyed Mary's view of the world and her own role in it, it seemed the only way she could ever hope to come to terms with her obsessive over-concern for the boy. Besides, Rick had to get away in order to find himself.

Was the childrearing aspect of their marriage more troublesome than any other? Probably not. What was different was the fact that he and Mary got along well all these years. There were no other major obstacles. It had been one of those high school romances that had actually worked.

Mary was truly a help-mate. She had been with him through the lean years as he struggled to establish himself in the business world. Content to be his complete alter ego, she had held the home together and given him the moral support he sorely needed during those trying times. She had never lost faith in him and continually encouraged him. The perfect hostess when required, he sometimes had to marvel at how she could come up with the appropriate remark, gesture, suggestion, as if reading his mind. They were a good team and he knew he owed no small measure of his success to her calm and steady influence.

He looked at his watch again. Almost eleven. Where were they? Should he call the police? Would he look foolish? Would they think him odd? Surely if there had been an accident they would have informed him at once. He couldn't believe the car had mechanical problems. Mary would have been on the phone immediately. He tried to concentrate on his project. He felt he would have made a good machinist if life had pointed him in that direction.

The doorbell rang. He hurried upstairs. Every step was more difficult, for he had a deep feeling of foreboding. In Korea he remembered he had the feeling many times. You could almost sense impending danger or disaster. He definitely had the feeling now. The bell rang again. He opened the door. There were two men standing there in business suits. One a little taller that the other. Funny what you notice at these times.

"Mr. Jason Knorr?" The taller man was addressing him. "I'm Lieutenant Donelly, Police Department. May we come in?"

Jason was overtaken by a dreadful anxiety despite an air about the speaker that was intended to impart calmness. He could detect compassion and understanding in the deep blue eyes that looked at him directly and openly, without a hint of guile in them. The other man with Donelly, although slightly shorter, also had that quiet look of efficiency and confidence that ordinarily would put one at ease.

Jason stood aside and indicated that they should enter. He led them into the living room and offered them seats. "Yes, I'm Jason Knorr. Something's happened, right?"

"Mr. Knorr, I know of no way to make this easy. We have

reason to believe your son, Rick Knorr, has had a fatal accident this evening." He watched Knorr carefully as he said this.

The man looked competent and intelligent. Even as he spoke, Donelly had the feeling, as he looked into Jason's slate blue eyes, that he could be a person of deep conviction, dedication and purpose. What he actually saw now was a deep hurt and a sudden flash of cognizance as the words he was speaking struck home.

Jason sat upright as if he had been yanked from above. The blood drained from his face and sweat poured from his forehead. He was numb, completely devastated. He had to collect his thoughts. Something was missing. In his confused mind he kept mulling over the words Donelly had told him. He couldn't get it together.

Donelly asked, concerned, "Are you all right? Can I do anything for you?"

The words snapped Jason back to the present; the pieces suddenly coming together, his mind clear and he knew what was next. He asked, "Was it an accident? How is my wife? Was she injured?"

Donelly turned sideways and threw a glance to Monero who was also instantly alert. "Your wife? I don't understand. We haven't a positive ID yet but we're certain it's your son. We'd like you to come down and try to identify his personal effects."

Jason looked at him with deep concern in his eyes and manner. "It's you who don't understand. My wife was with Rick. If there's been an accident I want to know where she is and how badly injured."

Donelly continued to stare. "It wasn't that type of accident. Your son was injured by firearms near a tobacco shop on the south side. He was alone as far as we know."

"No, no, no!" Jason shouted. "What about his car . . . my wife? I know he'd never have left his mother."

"Monero, get the license number and put it out on an All Points Bulletin. Maybe the second car."

A glance of instant understanding passed between them. The unidentified woman. Now Donelly realized that if his hunch were correct they would really be taking the measure of this man. A double tragedy could be devastating. In just the few short minutes he had been with Knorr there was something about him that evidenced an inner strength and stability that you didn't often see.

"I'm on it already," replied Monero, jumping for the phone located in the hallway. He returned a few minutes later and gave Donelly a nod.

Jason was getting it all put together in his mind now. He looked at the two detectives. "My wife had been shopping. Rick was supposed to pick her up around six or six-thirty. If Rick had failed to pick her up she would have called immediately." He sat, helplessly, waiting for some word of encouragement. Rick, dead. Christ, he just couldn't get it into his head. After all he had been through, to die in the street? Why?

Donelly watched Jason. He could sense the agony the guy must be going through, but he still had some business to conduct, a few more questions. He asked, "Do you know why your son would have stopped so far away from his usual area?" He was interrupted by the phone insistently ringing. Jason got up like a zombie to answer.

"It's for you Lieutenant." Donelly came over and took the phone. He listened intently for a few moments and took out his notebook. He gave Jason a strange look as he did so. He listened for some minutes more while writing feverishly in his notebook. Donelly finally hung up, turned, and returned to the living room, a look of deep concern and sympathy on his face. Monero recognized the somber look and expected the worst.

Immediately after returning to his seat, Donelly began: "Mr. Knorr, we've located your wife and also your son's car. I have some more unfortunate news for you. Apparently your wife was also a victim. She is at County General Hospital Emergency Room and is being treated for severe

17

injuries and shock. We can save any questions we have until later. I know you'll want to be with your wife right now. Rest assured we'll do everything possible to find the people responsible for all this." With that he motioned to Monero and they departed.

Monero's commented as they headed for the car, "Christ what a mess. You think he'll weather this okay?"

"I don't know. She's in severe shock and with the head injuries she received the Doctor feels she may never recover. But it's only a guess. She was really busted up inside. If she does live she'll be a vegetable for the rest of her life. It might be better all around if she doesn't make it. They won't know for sure until they complete further testing. It's a crummy break for him and his whole family." He then added, "Vince, there's something about this whole deal that smells. Get some feelers out on the street to see if we can come up with a reason. It's beginning to look more like a mistake to me."

"Roger, pardner. I'll get on it first thing in the morning."

4.

Jason sat in the living room for some minutes after the police had departed. The full impact of what he had been told was beginning to register on his consciousness. The magnitude of the entire tragedy was making it difficult to comprehend. He involuntarily gave a shudder. He had to pull himself together. What was it the policeman had said? Mary was at County General. He had to go to her at once. She would need him now more than at any time in their lives. Somehow they would put it all together. They had struggled through some hard times before.

He didn't bother to change before leaving for the hospital. There would be time for that later. He drove carefully. Even in his distressed state of mind he reverted to habit: the law-abiding citizen. Jason parked his car near the Emergency Room and entered the world of traumatic medicine. There were any number of people in the waiting room in various states of disarray. Some were injured, awaiting their turn. Others were people waiting in semi-shock for patients they had brought in for treatment. There were worried mothers and fathers with small children crying who had been injured at home. The noise and what appeared to be mass confusion was unnerving. He noticed all this as he approached the counter where a harassed-looking nurse was speaking on the telephone. She finally replaced the receiver and looked at him with a question on her face.

"I'm Jason Knorr. I was told you have my wife, Mary Knorr here somewhere." He looked at the nurse expectantly.

At first she didn't react, but she picked up a clip board and started going through the stack of forms clipped to it. At last she said, "Of course, Mr. Knorr. If you will go down the hall to Room 4 the doctor will be with you soon."

Jason followed the nurse's directions and entered the room. It was obviously a small office used for private conversations. He sat in one of the chairs and lit a cigarette. He needed something to calm his nerves and it also provided him with something to occupy his hands. He sat for what seemed like hours but actually was only a few minutes when the door opened and a very young looking man in a white coat entered. Jason's first impression was, "This can't be a doctor, he doesn't look any older than Rick."

The young man shook hands and said, "I'm Doctor Blier, a resident here at the hospital. I wanted to talk to you personally and try to prepare you before you see your wife. We have admitted her to the hospital intensive care unit and you may see her for a few minutes. Don't be surprised that she doesn't recognize you. She is, at present, aware of nothing about her. For her, time stopped when she witnessed the shooting of your son and was herself struck by the car. She was seriously injured by the accident. She has a crushed pelvis, a fracture of her arm and five ribs, and various internal injuries. However, the most serious injury by far was to her head when she struck the sidewalk. We placed her on life sustaining equipment immediately and the neurosurgeon will make his final evaluation in the morning. I must warn you, the prognosis is not good. Is there anything more I can tell you?"

It was obvious to Jason that the young man was busy and he appreciated the few quiet minutes he had taken to explain about Mary. He replied, "No, thank you, Doctor. I'd like to see Mary now if it's possible. I won't disturb her."

"Very well, the nurse will give you her room number. I'm sorry. I know how terrible this must be for you. If there is any way I can help you don't hestitate to call me." With that he got up and left the room, leaving Jason behind.

After a few moments Jason also left the room and returned to the nurses' station. After he obtained the room number and directions, he went to Mary's room. A nurse went with him. Mary lay on the bed, rigid, her eyes closed as if sleeping. She looked as if she were wired for sound. There were tubes and wires everywhere. There were monitors in a bank across a shelf above her bed. The nurse explained that her heart and breathing were being sustained by the equipment. She had strange brain wave patterns, but they wouldn't know the significance of that until the neurosurgeon was able to complete his tests in the morning. Then, a course of treatment could be started. Now the effort was to keep her body functioning. They would notify him at once of any diagnosis.

He spoke her name several times. No response. She gave no indication anyone was even in the room with her. He looked helplessly at the nurse and then walked from the room. He went slowly down the hallway, his mind still not completely clear or fully understanding the shattering of his entire life.

*   *   *

It was a couple of weeks later, and Rick's funeral a thing of the past. As a matter of fact, everything for Jason was a thing of the past. The head injuries Mary had received were just too massive. There was so much damage to the brain that she was unlikely to recover. They were transferring her to a permanent facility where they were prepared to sustain such comatose patients indefinitely, in Benson, some fifty miles away. She would probably remain there, as the doctor had told him, for the rest of her life. All tests, all treatments attempted had failed to reach her. Maybe in time she might come around but the doctor did not hold much hope for this.

The doctor had been very considerate and gentle in his explanation to Jason as to what exactly was wrong with his wife and why those at the hospital considered it hopeless. Even using the various life support systems, he ventured, "I'd say that within six to eighteen months, her condition would be terminal."

Everyone was sorry for Jason. He didn't want their pity or sympathy. He now lived for one thing—justice. The people who had shattered his life must be brought to pay for their crime. He had returned to work but it was apparent his heart wasn't in it any more. He tried, but the thought of the swine who did this had become a minor obsession with him. Perhaps after they were caught and punished he could settle down again.

He went to see Lieutenant Donelly a few weeks after Mary's transfer. The police had definitely decided it was a case of mistaken identity. Rick was possibly mistaken for a minor street hood named Barker, who disappeared immediately after the shooting. The word was out that he was wanted by certain people in the worst way. As a matter of fact, anyone knowing his whereabouts could maybe claim a little reward.

The Police Department had put out an All Points Bulletin on Barker but he appeared to have vanished. What they did know now was that Rick was the victim of a professional hit, but they weren't certain who had done it. The modus operandi suggested a couple of small-time hoods but there was no factual evidence yet that they were involved. If anything new turned up, Jason would be the first to know. When Jason asked, "What if nothing turned up," Donelly told him murder cases were never closed. They would stay on this until doomsday; the case would always be open. You never knew when a connection would be made and interest be regenerated. Jason said nothing.

Donelly never ceased feeling friendly toward Jason when talking with him. He knew from Jason's manner of speaking and his quiet composure that he would perservere and pressure until the criminals were caught. It was nothing he could put his finger on, but when you looked into those eyes you had the feeling they could turn into granite. They were honest and open, yes, but he felt they could close and become hard when the circumstances or situation demanded. He also felt that under the right conditions, Jason was a person he could relate closely to. There was a certain zest for life written in his face, and Donelly liked that.

The guy had lost a family. He wondered if he could endure the heartbreak this man was going through. He also realized that Knorr was putting his faith in the system, ex-pecting it to relieve some of his anguish by bringing the people who had harmed his wife and killed his son to justice. Donelly was also a family man—also loved his wife dearly—so he could emphasize with Jason.

Jason left the meeting and returned to his home to think. He'd been doing a lot of that lately.

5.

Marco Benotti sat at his desk, the cup of coffee near his right hand, untouched as yet. The desk was completely bare except for a telephone, ashtray, and a pen and pencil set built into a lamp base. The desk was so highly polished that it seemed to glow. He had a long panatela cigar wedged between the first two fingers of his right hand. It was always there. He used it to emphasize points in his conversations much as an instructor would use a pointer.

He sat in a large leather chair. The office itself was richly but conservatively furnished. It could have been any executive's office with the desk cleared for action.

The man sitting across the desk from him seemed to feel out of place and was extremely agitated. At last Benotti spoke to him, "It's been a few weeks and I still haven't been satisfied. If you hadn't screwed up, this would all be over. You've caused me a lot of embarrassment and heat from the police. I don't like that kind of attention."

Joe Peroni sat and listened in silence. He had a long way to go to get back into, the good graces of the Organization. He'd always been a good soldier. Christ, this was the first time he'd ever goofed any assignment. He had to admit it had been a lulu.

Benotti continued. "I want Barker. I want his head on a platter and I want it quick. This guy couldn't completely disappear. Someone had to see and hear something. He'll have to eventually contact an old friend or someone. He's not the type to survive long on his own. I want you to make this your pet project. Stay on it till you find him."

Peroni listened. How would he explain to Angela that he might have to leave for a few days or weeks? He'd have to have a cover, money, and most of all, he'd be away from the kids. He sighed. A job was a job and this one he had to finish. All he said was, "I will do as you ask. I'm sorry I have caused any embarrassment." He then got up and left. As he

24

left the outer office he was handed an envelope: the necessary funds to continue the search.

*   *   *

Cliff Barker woke up in a dingy motel room. He had slept fitfully and now his eyes were grainy and his mouth felt like the Russian Army had been marching through it. He looked over at the stupid hick bimbo he had shared his bed with. He wondered idly why all these small-town bimbos always liked to make it with guys from the big time. All he had to do was let the chick know he was Somebody in the big city and she had been ready for a roll. Well, it was now time to kick her ass out; he had to be alone for a while. So far, so good. Maybe he'd be lucky and get away clean. He knew they would look for him at first, but then they would give up, for he wasn't that important.

After he'd left the city everyone would think he headed for Mexico. He'd driven south for a hundred or so miles and sold his car for cash. He hadn't gotten much, but it was better than nothing. He had then back-tracked to the city and headed east. They would never look for him here. He did have one problem. He was starting to run out of money. He'd have to come up with something pretty soon. The thought of working never entered his mind. If it had, he would only have rejected the thought. His type scorned any honest work as being only for the clods. After he got rid of the broad he'd think of something. He went into the bathroom to wash his face and hands.

*   *   *

The police received word about the sale of Barker's car from the Bureau of Motor Vehicles. Benotti found out through the same sources almost as soon as Donelly and Monero. He passed the information on to Peroni for checking and verification. Donelly had Monero travel to Silver City to make sure it had indeed been Barker who sold the car and to gather any other information he could get from the locals. He would go himself but so many cases were building up it was hard to get away. He wouldn't have gone

25

to this much trouble but he felt he owed Jason Knorr. It galled him they couldn't get a lead on the killers. Barker might just be the answer. Peroni had dropped from circulation also. This fit into the overall concept of what had happened a few weeks earlier. He'd just have to wait till Monero returned.

6.

Jason sat in the family room of his home watching television. It still seemed so strange to him to sit there alone. Mary would not be there in her chair if he looked. She will never return, never sit there again, he thought. No clatter or noise from upstairs either. Rick's stereo no longer filled the house with music. He tried to concentrate on the television show but his attention was continually diverted by his thoughts. It just wasn't working. He had to get away for a while. But where? Perhaps he could move to Benson; being close to Mary might, in some way, help her. Maybe someday she would respond to his voice, his touch. Yet he also knew such thoughts were useless. The doctors had been emphatic on this point.

He thought about Rick. He had a lot of fond memories of the boy when he was young. They'd had a lot of fun together. Since he was an only child they had been able to spend a lot of time together. He reminisced about some of the family vacations they had taken, with Mary being a little over-protective but not overbearing.

How Rick had changed after his tour in Vietnam! After he returned he was subject to rapid mood changes. It seemed almost everything at one time or another irritated him. Mary had tried to find the little boy in him again but that was lost forever. Jason tried getting through to him with tales of his own wartime experiences and, it appeared to Jason, that Rick was just finding himself again when this catastrophe occurred.

The more he thought about Mary and Rick and the circumstances causing his death and her living death, the more he had to admit he was not completely happy with the way the police were handling the case. He realized that this case was not the only one they were dealing with and knew he had to have patience. He didn't know why, but he had a lot of confidence in Lieutenant Donelly. The man had that quiet self-assurance that made you feel you could trust him completely. Jason had appreciated the time he had extended to explain to him what they were doing, but his patience was nonetheless wearing thin. He wanted justice for his family and he wanted it soon.

A few months had now passed. The trip Sergeant Monero had made to Silver City had been fruitless. Barker had been there, but the trail had petered out. The case was now on the back burner, but would remain open to be cross-referenced from time to time with similar crimes. He felt no satisfaction from this knowledge. He knew the police had done all they could under the circumstances. As a matter of fact, Lieutenant Donelly had given him considerable background and more information than he normally would have in such cases. He had also read some old newspapers and had asked others about what sort of people would do such things. At this point it was idle curiosity; just a desire to know more.

He had heard several names mentioned in their conversations. Jason had listened to Lieutenant Donelly carefully, but at the time the names had been meaningless. The name Marco Benotti was one that appeared in the paper from time to time. Benotti was in some way connected with organized crime—the numbers racket he remembered. Benotti was linked to other criminal activities as well, but the store where Rick had been gunned down had been a collection point for numbers and that's what had stuck in his memory. Lieutenant Donelly had also mentioned other names of people who supposedly worked for Benotti, but at the time they slipped his mind. What real difference did it make? Lieutenant Donelly felt if they could catch up with the runner, Barker, they might have the key and could find out which of Benotti's men had been involved. That Benotti was somehow responsible seemed clear, but proof of this was something else.

Jason shifted his thoughts. No use worrying about what you can't change. Starting tomorrow, I'll sort through Rick's things and dispose of what I can. The thought of disposal made him consider the house. I should sell it, move out; it's much too large for me now. Too many memories here. Of course if I do that, then I'll have to dispose of Mary's personal items too. I don't know if I can. I'll go away for a while. Perhaps when I return I can think about it more objectively. He looked at his watch. My God, it's so late. I didn't eat again. I'll have a sandwich and go to bed. Tomorrow I must talk with Sanders. Maybe I'll just quit and move up to Benson. He got up, turned off the television and headed for the kitchen.

7.

The call came about 2:30 A.M. Bonnie had been sound asleep and difficult to awaken. She had been out all evening and was still a little drugged from all the alcohol she had consumed. That Artie was really something else. It took a minute or so to register just who she was talking to on the phone. When she did she sat up in bed, alert and ready to listen. The voice on the phone belonged to Cliff Barker.

"Baby, I'm desperate and need your help." She could barely hear him, his voice was muffled, but she knew it was him.

"Where are you? I've missed you so much," she replied.

"I know, I miss you too, that's why I'm calling. I know I can trust you to do as I ask. You do this for me and we'll go away together somewhere." He could picture her in his mind, half asleep, those big, beautiful boobs just hanging out there to be fondled. The thought excited him; it took all his concentration to get back to business.

She had to tell him. "Cliff, honey, they're looking for you high and low. It's not safe for you anywhere. They came around to see me after you'd left, but I told them I didn't know anything. I don't know if they believed me, but they left."

"That's my Baby. Now, listen carefully. In your cellar storage room is an old suitcase. You remember, the one I used when I moved in with you? I want you to bring it to me tomorrow night. Can you do that?"

She thought very quickly. Christ, what a mess. On the phone she said, "Of course, I'll go down and get it right away. Where should I bring it?"

"Baby, I'm really depending on you. I'll meet you on the corner of 5th and Elm at 11 P.M. Be ready to travel. Just bring yourself; we'll get anything you need later."

"Are you in the city now? Why don't you just come here?"

He replied immediately. "They may be watching you.

They know you're my lady. I can't take the chance. Just be careful and make sure you're not followed."

"All right, tomorrow night then." She hung up the phone. Fully awake now, she realized she had to do some thinking. First things first, she thought. She got up and dressed. She had to find the suitcase.

She left her room and went down the stairs to the basement. Each apartment had a small wire cage in the basement for the storage of rarely used items. She opened the padlock and went inside. It only took a couple of minutes until she uncovered the old, battered valise. It wasn't heavy. What could be in here so important he'd take such risks to get it back? She had no illusions about her status with Cliff. She was good looking and handy; that's all that they had between them. She took the valise back to her apartment and set it down in the living room. It certainly didn't look like much. The more she looked at it, the more her curiosity was aroused. It was locked. It was also very old. Should she open it or not? The desire to look inside was overpowering.

Curiosity finally overcame her fear. Taking a knife, she slit the side of the bag. Looking inside, all she could find was a brown paper sack which she opened. It was full of money. She almost fainted. Sweat broke out on her forehead. She was now so frightened she could hardly think. After a few minutes, she had calmed down a little. She counted the money, mostly in hundred dollar bills. There was eighteen thousand, three hundred dollars in the sack. What she could do with that much money! She had never seen that much before and she had all sorts of fantasies in the next few minutes. Then the old fear came back and gripped her tightly around the chest.

She started thinking. She was in the clear with everyone. Now he had to come back and drag her into his problems. He had no right. They would never leave him alone and once they knew she was with him and helped him, she would be in the same boat with him. It was unfair, but what

31

could she do? Cliff might beat her, or worse, once in awhile. He was unpredictable. But the Organization had a long memory and a long arm. Would she ever be safe? Bonnie finally convinced herself she would not be.

All that money lying on the coffee table had practically mesmerized her. She went into the kitchen to make coffee, all thought of sleep now gone. She knew what she had to do. Greed and the instinct for survival had taken over completely.

8.

The next morning, Jason went in to talk with his boss. He explained the difficulties he was having with his adjustment. He thought it best he quit. He wanted to move nearer to Mary. Bob Sanders was very sympathetic. Jason had worked for him for years, in fact was his best salesman. Together they had made quite a team and had been very successful money-wise. He didn't want Jason to quit.

"Take a few weeks off, Jason. Get away for a while. When you feel like it, your job will be here. Don't move just yet; give yourself some more time."

Jason thought it over for a few minutes and said he'd let him know. He was just not sure staying here was the best idea. He had to try and help Mary if he could. He also wanted to be around when the police finally found the people responsible. He returned home, packed a few things, then left for Benson where he'd rent a motel room for a couple of weeks. He was beginning to feel cheated by life. He had always been the fair one, straight and narrow, always done his duty without complaining. His life had been completely uprooted because of someone else, and he felt they should be punished. He had listened to Lieutenant Donelly, he had listened to his minister, he had listened to the doctors. Did it make a difference? Hell no.

Sometimes, he was so lonely he thought he'd lose his sanity. He had to rest, he had to think the problem through, he had to adjust. The two weeks with Mary might be just what he needed. He arrived at Benson late in the evening. After checking into his motel he felt hungry for the first time in days. Maybe it was the close proximity of Mary. His feelings were buoyed. Tomorrow he'd visit her. Who knows, maybe this was the start on her recovery. He went to the dining room with a sprightly gait.

9.

Later that same morning Marco Benotti, sitting in his office, received a mysterious phone call. Undisturbed, he listened to the caller. He was accustomed to this type of call. Some frightened little weasel would be around later with his hand out. There had been something odd about the call, he thought later. He was almost certain it had been a woman, even though the voice had been muffled. He really wasn't concerned though, for the message was the important item.

He, in turn, called a number on his private line. Joe Peroni answered almost at once. "Our bird has returned to his nesting ground. He will be at 5th and Elm tonight at 11 P.M. I thought you might want to give him a personal welcome home."

Peroni answered quickly. "I'll certainly look into the matter. It would be unkind not to welcome back an old friend." With that he hung up, for he had a lot of preparations before his evening appointment.

By 3 P.M. he had his team reconstituted and they were sitting in Joe's car near the meeting place. They decided to leave Mike nearby the rest of the day, out of sight, but where he could observe activity. After Mike left, Joe and Tony drove back to Tony's place to wait. Tonight should wrap up their problem. They were both acutely aware that another failure would zero them out.

*   *   *

At 10 P.M. Cliff approached the rendezvous corner cautiously. He wanted to observe anyone nearby and decided he would take up a position at 6th and let Bonnie show up first. Let her sweat a little; she'd appreciate him more. He had already made plans to dump her after he got his bag. He stood in a darkened doorway, watching the intersection of 5th and Elm.

*   *   *

Gallagher had spotted him immediately as he walked down Elm, approaching from 7th Street. At one point, he could have reached out and touched him. The temptation had been great, but he had to wait for Joe and Tony. They should be here any time. He heard the tapping on the concrete and left his place of concealment to walk around the corner. The other two were there and he gave them Barker's location. "Pretty cagey ain't he, coming down to case the area. This time it won't do him any good. We got him dead to rights."

As Gallagher approached, Barker sensed danger, but several people had already walked past with no problem. He didn't recognize him, so he relaxed a little. Too late, he sensed the presence behind him. He started to turn but they were on him like hungry wolves on a sheep. They forced him back into the doorway. Joe had his hand on Barker's mouth and his body weight forced him backwards. Barker's head struck the door, his eyes widening with terror as he looked at Joe and felt his excited hot breath blowing on his face. He could barely see the man on his left who grabbed his hair. Then the lights went out as Tony forced the ice pick into his left ear. It had all taken seconds as Barker's body stiffened and then went slack. The three took another look up and down the street and hurried away into the darkness. Other than a couple of grunts, no noise or commotion had occurred. No one had seen or heard anything.

*   *   *

The next day, as Lieutenant Donelly came on duty, the computer made another connection for him. He didn't like what he read. A body found by a roving patrol car had been identified and routine checking through old cases had cross-referenced his name for Donelly. It was Cliff Barker. So they had got him after all. He must have been a complete fool to return to the city. Why? He'd run a check on it but he knew the answer already. He'd discover nothing.

*   *   *

That afternoon, Bonnie was on a bus heading east into the desert country. Driven by fear, she could only hope they wouldn't look for, or didn't know about the money.

10.

Jason spent the next week in Benson. He never deviated from his daily routine. Up early, he ate breakfast in the motel dining room before going to the hospital. He would spend the morning reading to Mary aloud from some of her old favorite and time-worn stories. He would eat lunch in the cafeteria and then wait until she had completed her daily sponge bath. All the while, he was talking and stroking her, hoping against hope she might respond. In the evenings he would return to the motel, watch a little television, then go to bed.

The nurses and other attendants had taken notice of the visits. It was heart-rending to see him daily, so full of hope, only to leave in the evening worn out from the constant physical and mental strain. In the middle of the second week the doctor called him into his office and had a chat with him. He pointed out what must be evident, that Mary was making no progress and he was only harming himself. It would be best all around for him to pick up the pieces of his life and start anew and to leave Mary in the hands of the professionals. He gave him no hope, only that they would continue caring for her until she either recovered or the situation worsened. In any event, he would be notified at once.

That night, after supper, Jason came into her room. It would be the last time, at least for a while. He had decided to follow the doctor's advice and return to the city. He sat holding her hand. He talked to her quietly and earnestly for perhaps two hours, recalling their young love, of how happy they had been with little Rick, the house, everything he could think of, but it was no use. He had tried to force his health into her by his intensity of emotion but it didn't work. Helplessly, he looked at her. God, she was beautiful, so small and innocent, how happy she had made him. Tears started down his cheeks, uncontrolled, and he let them quietly slide down his face. He could taste the bitter salt but paid it no heed. Suddenly, he shuddered, pulled himself upright and said, "Goodbye my love. We'll never cry again. I love you." Then he got up and slowly left the room, not looking back. He had things to do.

The next morning he drove back to the city. He was still unsure of what to do. He had to get himself organized. Life continued even through hardship and heartache. Arriving home he picked up an accumulation of mail and old newspapers from his next door neighbor and went through the letters over a cup of coffee. Nothing important, a few bills, an advertisement or two. He'd have to cancel a couple of subscriptions. On his second cup of coffee he started through the papers. He organized them by date and began skimming through them. It was old news and he only wanted the highlights to bring himself up to date.

He almost dropped his coffee cup. Inside, on page two, he read of the death of Cliff Barker. The name leapt at him from the page. He read the details slowly, not wanting to miss a word. It was a typical professional hit, according to police. He had been wanted in connection with several crimes, but that was all. He hurriedly went through the rest of the stack of papers, but no more reference was made to Barker or to the crime. It was unbelievable. Surely they had done more than note the passing of some gangster. They must have investigated it thoroughly. He then thought of Lieutenant Donelly. He'd go see him. He would help.

He ate lunch, washed up, and then drove down to the police station. This time he had a little trouble getting by the desk sergeant, but he finally let him go up to homocide. He came into an office where confusion would have been an understatement. Lieutenant Donelly motioned him to come into his office. After he sat down, Donelly started right in.

"You can see we're rather busy, Mr. Knorr, but I can give you a few minutes. Every nut in the city has decided to become active at once. This place has been a madhouse since I came on duty this morning. What can I do for you?"

Jason asked, "I saw in the papers Cliff Barker was found dead. I'd like to know if you've found out anything further about my son's killers?"

Lieutenant Donelly shook his head negatively. "We never had a chance to talk with him. They got to him first. Although your son's case will remain open, I'm afraid it will join the legion of unsolved homicides. We have them stored in cases downstairs."

Jason looked at him unbelievingly. This couldn't be happening to him. He said, "You told me a few weeks ago you had a hunch, you mentioned some names; doesn't that mean anything?"

Lieutenant Donelly looked at him for a few seconds and made up his mind. "Mr. Knorr, I'm going to tell you what I think, and then I'm closing the case out unsolved. I know it won't help, but maybe it'll make you feel better. There's a fellow in town named Marco Benotti who controls almost every racket known to man. He has hundreds of people working for him; Barker was only one. There is only one way to keep these people in line—fear. He also has several specialists in this category, namely, three men named Calucci, Peroni and Gallagher. What I think happened is that Barker got caught stealing and was set up for execution. He looked enough like your son for them to make a mistake in the rain. Later, Barker came back for some unknown reason and they didn't miss on the second try. Who actually did it is anyone's guess. Because of the past history of three of his people, who I mentioned to you before and who work together, we brought them all in for questioning. But they all had alibis. We did learn Barker's old girlfriend departed town the same day Barker was murdered. She disappeared into the woodwork."

Jason sat for a few seconds mulling this all over. It's just like the movies: gangland hit, no witnesses and everyone is covered. He was starting to get a little edgy. Lieutenant Donelly watched him closely. He didn't like the look in his eyes. Suddenly Jason jumped up. "It's not fair. You mean to tell me two men have been murdered, my wife . . . has been destroyed, my life has been turned into a shambles and you're going to do nothing? For Christ's sake, Lieutenant, where's justice?" He was now prowling back and forth in front of Donelly's desk.

Donelly stood up. "Mr. Knorr, the police have to work with evidence. We don't like it but those are the rules. We fight a battle every day out there in that jungle. Sometimes we win, sometimes we lose, but we have to stick to the rules."

Jason had calmed down. As suddenly as his outburst had begun, it ended. "I'm sorry, Lieutenant, I had no right to talk like that. I know you did your best. Thank you." He then turned and left the office. Case closed. Everyone was returning to routine. Life must go on.

After Jason left, Donelly sat for some time thinking about him. For a moment he'd seen those eyes of his go hard as stone. He had met any number of people like Knorr, good law-abiding citizens until provoked. Even after he'd calmed down after his outburst there had remained something in those eyes that indicated some kind of decision had been made during those few seconds. He wasn't sure he liked what he was thinking. His incipient ulcer started growling at him and he reached for another cigarette. He thought to himself, "One of these days, I'm going to give this business up."

In all his meetings with Knorr he had been impressed with the man. He could tell by Knorr's reaction to him that the feeling was mutual. He could feel (or imagined he could feel) the way Knorr felt about the dead-end police in- vestigation. If the situation were reversed, he might feel and react the same way. What if it were my family? How would I handle this? How would I react to the stimulus of wanting justice and being frustrated? Would it be rage, depression, or something else? It all depended on your point of view.

*   *   *

That night, Jason sat in his family room. There was

40

something just not right about this situation. People did not go around killing other people with complete impunity. Or did they? He let this question roll around his mind for awhile. It was an interesting conjecture. If he wanted to kill, what would he do, how would he do it? "Vengeance is mine, sayeth the Lord," but sometimes He can use a little help. He thought of several ways, rejecting them one by one. The thought of killing another was repugnant to him, even though he had done it before. Hell, twenty or so years ago they had given him a couple of medals for it. He'd been rather proficient at his job at that time. He wondered if the same old skill, agility, and cunning were still there.

*   *   *

The next morning he called a realtor. He wanted to sell his house. After that, he went by a storage warehouse and arranged to store some of the household furnishings. The rest he would try to sell. He resigned from his job with Sanders and told him he was moving to Benson or some other nearby city. He disposed of the second car, the one his wife used to drive. He cleaned out everything. In leaving the city, he wanted to sever it completely. He had a plan which he considered well-thought out. Maybe it wasn't foolproof, but in life there are seldom sure things.

He held a garage sale a few days later. Many of the small items he was able to dispose of at that time. The furniture was fine, well-built, well cared- for. It also went fairly fast. Then came the day he sold the house. It almost broke his heart. This is it, he thought, the final tie. Once it's broken there will be no turning back. He drove to Benson and rented a post office box. He would need a place to receive mail for a while. It would soon dry up, but for now he needed it. He also went to the local bank and rented a safety deposit box. This was essential to his plan. Finally, he rented a room for a couple of weeks at the motel. Now he was ready. He counted his assets. With the sale of the house, plus savings, it came to nearly $120,000.

The day after he closed on the sale of the house, he drove

41

to Benson. He placed his insurance policies and other important papers in the safety deposit box along with half the money in cash. He made arrangements with the post office to stack his mail until he called for it just in case the P.O. box he rented would not hold it all. He wanted, if possible, to cover every base. After accomplishing these details he sat down and wrote out his proposed plan. He also wrote out a simple will and had it notarized at the Bank of Benson. He placed all this, except for one copy of the will, in the safety deposit box. He sealed the last copy in an envelope and gave it to his lawyer, to be opened only if he were reported dead by any means. His attorney didn't like it, but he complied with Jason's wish. After all, it was only a will.

He drove back to Benson from the city. He was pretty sure he had everything he needed. His next step would be important. Once made, he was absolutely committed to his plan. He stayed at the motel for three days, each day driving out to the countryside, looking. After another day of searching, he decided he had to go further afield. A week after he left the city he was back. There would be more anonymity in a large city than there would be in Benson or one of the other smaller towns or villages in the area. He went to a bank in a completely unfamiliar section of the city and rented another safety deposit box. In it, he placed the remaining half of his money, keeping only enough cash on hand for short-term expenses. He rented this second box under the name Donald Roberts. Roberts had been with him in Korea and had bought the farm, so it was a safe name. He realized a persistent search would find him but all he needed was a few months or a year, and it wouldn't matter any longer. He rented a small apartment in a dingy building not far from the bank. The landlord liked to deal in cash and so did "Roberts."

After he settled into his new apartment, he bought an older model car, paying cash, and registered it under his new name. He also applied for a driver's license. This was a risk, but since Don had been dead for so long, the chances

42

were slim any check would go that far back. After getting his car, he drove north to another large city and rented another room for a week. The next day, he began his search of the pawn shops and gun dealers. He was looking for a particular combination in a weapon, for he felt he had to stay with something familiar.

During his three years of service in the Army he had been in the infantry. In Korea, they had taken him and a few other selected men and gave them special training. They had trained Jason to be a sniper. This was highly specialized training and had been done with especially equipped rifles. He had become very proficient, the best in his class. He knew every characteristic and function of his weapon. An expert rifleman even before he joined up, they had honed his skills to a fine edge. They had taught him how to search out targets and taught him concealment. Jason was an excellent student. He had personally accounted for 23 enemy troops that were confirmed and twice that number of probables. They had given him a medal and sent him home. He hadn't thought about or used those skills since. And what he was planning now was entirely different. This time there would be no medals.

*   *   *

The first day he bought a cartridge reloader. He also purchased a few minor items he would need to load his own ammunition. He had made his purchase here because they didn't have his weapon and he wanted to spread the sales over a broad area. He also went into a large chain drug store and bought a jar of Vaseline, a couple of packages of gum and two pairs of surgeon's gloves. He also purchased Preparation H suppositories in case he was asked why he needed the gloves. After he left the drug store, he threw away everything but the gloves and vaseline.

Two days later he found his weapon. It was quite by chance, for the place was so seedy he almost passed it up. The minute the salesman handed it to him, he knew this was it. It was a 1903 model Springfield and scope. The weapon just fit in his hand. Twenty or more years melted away and he was nineteen again. He worked the mechanism. Perfect. He checked out the bore. Whoever had owned it before had given it loving care, for the bore was clean as a whistle. In fact, the entire weapon looked like it was in mint condition. The telescope was clean and well cared-for also. It and the rifle were immediately like old friends; he knew them both intimately. All the training he had undergone so long ago came flooding back. He bought the weapon on the spot, not even haggling over the price.

He then went to a sporting goods store and bought a small tent, sleeping bag, stove, and other camping supplies. He also purchased 200 rounds of 30.06 caliber ammunition to take with him. The ammunition, making sure to get the same brand, he bought in three different stores so the amount wouldn't attract attention. He felt he was now ready. The next day he checked out of his room and returned to his own city. His apartment needed cleaning so he set about it with a vengeance and rapidly completed the task. He wanted nothing to interfere with his concentration for the next few days.

After he finished cleaning he set up his reloader on the kitchen table, got all his other equipment together plus the ammunition, and started working. He separated each cartridge and carefully weighed each charge. He made sure, before reloading, that each round had the exact amount of charge. He added a little here, removed some there, and, after a couple of days, had 175 rounds of perfectly matched ammunition. Next, he turned his attention to the scope. He cleaned it, checked all the mountings to see that they would be secure: no stripped screws, clamps in good order. He went to one of the city parks, wanting to leave nothing to chance, and, within two days, calibrated his scope. He was now ready for the rifle itself.

He disassembled it completely, making sure it was perfect. He went over each part individually, down to the last screw and spring, checking for worn or broken parts.

He had been right in the little shop. The weapon was immaculate. He purchased a new stock and in the local crafts shop reworked it to where it fit his body configuration perfectly. The cheek rest and length fit him like a glove. He was now ready for testing. He was able to disassemble the weapon and scope into three parts for easier handling. The next day, he would be ready.

11.

The sun was streaming throught the trees, casting oblong shafts of light onto the still gloomy forest floor. The Hunter was already up building a morning fire. The tent flaps were open allowing the inner tent to be aired out. There was a little chill in the early morning air but he knew in an hour or so the sun would warm it nicely. It would be another perfect day. A few more and it would be time to head for home. The month here in the mountains and forests had done him a world of good, he thought to himself. He had lost at least ten pounds, his skin was now a deep bronze from the sun and wind, he looked great and felt terrific. His slate-blue eyes seemed clear and hard as he looked at them in the mirror while shaving. His face told him he'd taken years off; the deep worry lines he'd developed were gone. Once he'd made his decision a certain tranquility and serenity of purpose had come over him. He had his basic plan thought out but now he had to return to put it into action. He had to determine its scope and intensity, had to fine-tune it, in a word.

He had thought it all over carefully. He had been convinced that Gallagher, Callucci, and Peroni had been the people responsible for his personal catastrophe. That they must face his retribution, there was no question. Since he could not determine who might have actually done the shooting, all must die.

This was the start of a deeper, more soul-searching consideration. Should he include anyone else? What of the one who gave the orders? He decided to delay that decision until the time came. He would first have to be successful in eliminating the three killers. He realized that he had to draw the line somewhere or his vendetta would take on impossible proportions. There was no way possible he could fight the entire system and expect to win.

He had also made up his mind as to the order of their elimination. His list was tentative. He still wanted to study each of them, in turn, before making his move against them. He also had to consider counter-moves against him by the Organization. Having thought the problem through, he felt confident he could get one or two before they realized it was a deliberate attack upon them. This would be the overriding consideration on whether to continue after eliminating the three soldiers. After them, he would have to reassess his position in light of that future situation.

The first week, he had constructed himself a known-distance rifle range. He had carefully marked off 200, 300, and 500 yards, and then carefully zeroed his rifle and scope at each distance, noting the settings for each range. He had purposely waited each day until there was a minimum effect from the wind, in order to get a true setting for his scope. The matched ammunition he'd made worked perfectly. He knew it would all along, for he had been one of the best. The month in the mountains had resharpened his skills. He hadn't forgotten much of his previous training.

Today, he would finish his 500-yard firing. His target was a ten-inch square sheet of paper. Not much to aim at from that distance, but it was approximately the size of the target he'd be firing at. In a few days he'd head back to the city and start his final preparations. He cleaned everything up around the campsite, doused the fire and headed toward his homemade range.

He went downrange first and put up his target, placing it roughly head high on the tree trunk. Satisfied that he had it tacked up solidly, he started uprange. As he covered the distance, he carefully looked around. He was all alone. Even if someone came up, he could say he was getting his new rifle ready for the hunting season. It would be the complete truth. He smiled at that thought, one of the first smiles he'd cracked in weeks. Arriving at his firing position, he started his final preparations, assumed the prone position and made the last adjustments on his sling. He loaded the rifle with three rounds and engaged the safety. Peering into his scope, he scanned downrange. With no one between him and his target, the rifle finally came to rest pointing on target. He relaxed a moment, released the safety and reassumed his firing position. The cross hairs of his scope now marked the center of the target. He slowly took up the slack on his trigger and with steady pressure continued to squeeze. The rifle suddenly bucked, the recoil being absorbed comfortably by his shoulder, but a split-second later the rifle was again lined up on the target. He repeated the manuever two more times. The rounds fired had been 19, 20 and 21 at this range.

He walked up to his target. Not dead center, but he had a respectable shot group you could cover with a coffee mug. Not bad, he thought. Not quite as good as the old days, but not bad. Soon he'd be ready to head back, for he felt as ready as he'd ever be. It was time for the hunt.

That evening, after he had finished eating, he cleaned all his utensils. The ritual had become almost second nature to him during his stay on the hillside. Each night he had to hang his food and clear all his leftovers to ensure that wild animals would not be attracted to his campsite. After completing the cleanup, darkness had finally come; the only light was that which was provided by his flickering campfire. He listened quietly to his portable radio and cleaned and oiled his rifle by the light of the fire. He was completely at peace with the world. No one would believe his intent as he sat there alone in the woods. He decided he'd return to the range the next day and recheck his sight settings at each range one more time. He wanted to be absolutely certain. Once started, there would be no margin for error. At last he completed his cleaning chore and prepared for bed.

* * *

A few days later he was sitting in his apartment looking through the telephone book. He wrote down the home addresses of all the M. Gallagher's, J. Peroni's, and A. Callucci's. He couldn't find Benotti in the book. No matter. From the papers he knew where his office was located. His conversations with Donelly and the newspaper accounts made it clear that Benotti owned a couple of supper clubs which he could also check out. Sitting there, after writing down the names, he thought, "There has to be more. I want them to know. I want them to sweat." After a considerable amount of time he went to his dictionary. He looked up a couple of words and his idea jelled. The Queen of Spades would be his calling card. The Queen would represent his wife, the Spade suit from the deck would represent the broadsword. He would become the Queen's sword of vengeance.

After making his selection of a calling card, he savored the effect that receiving the card would have on the person getting it. To the first man he realized it would make no difference whatsoever. As he moved up the line, however, the others would become aware of the significance and he hoped it would instill, if not terror, at least fear in them. At every step of the way he would insure that no innocent person would be harmed by his action. Right now, he had to identify his targets.

The next day he started his eliminations. He went through the Caluccis until he narrowed it to two possibilities. By that evening he had observed them both and, on a hunch, he followed the younger of the two. He followed him for two days until about 8:00 P.M., on the second night, when he walked into one of Benotti's supper clubs. Bingo. Jason followed his man inside the club. At first, he didn't see his quarry, but at last picked him out sitting near the front with another man. He found an empty bar stool and ordered a beer. From time to time he glanced around the bar and dining room. He ordered another beer. The two men were at ease, having a drink, and completely engrossed in their conversation. The Hunter just sat; he was getting used to sitting and watching. After an hour the two broke up and left the bar. Jason followed casually and on intuition followed the second man. After driving across town the man pulled into a driveway, locked his car and went into the house. It was obvious to the hunter that the

49

man was home. He looked at his list. Zero. The address wasn't on his list. But at least he had Calucci identified. He would just have to bide his time.

The next morning he was up early. He went to one of the city parks and jogged for awhile. He had to keep up his conditioning for the long haul, for he had embarked on a dangerous scheme. Once it got going he'd have Donelly after him as well as the Organization. He wasn't too concerned. If he could get his licks in he'd be satisfied. He hoped and thought he had it planned so that he'd be able to walk away, but the "best laid plans of mice and men... ." Now that he had Calucci located and identified he'd start on the next one.

That afternoon he worked his way through the Gallaghers. Christ, why did all Irishmen have to be named Mike. He finally narrowed it down to three. The next few days he'd follow them in turn until he found the right one. After tracking one Mike for two days, he satisfied himself that this one was strictly a family man. He didn't go out at night. The second one worked at a car dealership and was single. The third, Jason also eliminated because he was a factory worker and this didn't fit into his concept of an Organization man. He concentrated on the second one. He appeared to be in his mid-thirties and was darkly handsome. The Hunter cataloged him dispassionately; about 6 feet tall, 180 pounds, athletic and quick. He'd be a real trophy to bring down. He observed him for a few days and at last he was rewarded. Gallagher went to the same supper club as Calucci had gone to earlier. This time, however, Jason stayed outside, for he didn't want to get too well known by anyone. Nor did he want to risk a chance recognition by an old acquaintance. Eventually, he put Gallagher to bed and then went home himself.

The following day was devoted to running down the third hit man. Things must be quiet, he thought; the three haven't met or talked with each other since he started his observations. Perhaps they only came together when they had a job to do. He started through the Peronis in the telephone directory. He found the right one immediately, following him to a big estate in the suburbs which he knew to be the home of Marco Benotti. Obviously, this Peroni had no real job. Jason was sure, now, that he had one of the killers without doubt. It would be nice if he could connect the other two with this guy. When Peroni went back home that evening he was met by a little boy, maybe seven years old. There was also a beaming wife and small girl aged two or three. It almost broke the Hunter's resolve. He hadn't planned on this, yet it made no difference. He would follow through with his plan. Having spotted them all, it was time to go to work.

The next day he dressed carefully. He drove up to Benson. He wanted to check his mail box. He arrived at the post office and, as Jason Knorr, picked up his mail. He had been right. There was only a little mail for him; final notes, paid in full receipts, etc. After reading them, he placed the important ones in his safety deposit box; the rest he destroyed. Then he returned to the city. On the way back he made two stops, purchasing two decks of playing cards at each stop.

*   *   *

The Hunter stalked his quarry for two weeks. He followed him everywhere. He put him to bed each night and was there in the morning to take him to work. Except for the nights he went out with a couple of different women, he stayed pretty well in a routine. He had picked Gallagher because he was single and mobile. If anyone panicked, it would be either Gallagher or Calucci, they could pull up stakes and leave; the other one was married and more likely to sit. After the second week, Gallagher had set up a pattern. There was one night, Thursday, that he went to Benotti's supper club. So this would be it. He now had to get his blind set up. He spent the next week checking out the entire neighborhood. He looked it over during the day as well as after dark. He spent three nights just observing

51

the club and its parking lot. He noted everything. There was a patrol car, the same one every night. He checked its time and route on two successive nights. Like everyone else, the police had a set routine for covering their area. What he needed was a safe access and an escape route. The escape route would be the most important. He wanted at least two, two main ones and an emergency back-up in case anything went wrong or he was blocked from his primary escape. He also wanted the target in an area of good visibility and background. Night firing would be a little difficult but he wasn't worried.

After scouting the area for a couple of days, he finally found a spot he thought suitable. He would spend several more nights making absolutely sure it would fit all requirements. It was an old loft in a building two blocks from the supper club parking lot. He spent a portion of the next two nights investigating the building. From his vantage point he had a clear view of almost the entire parking lot. He checked with binoculars, observing traffic and visibility. The lot was well lit. Yes, this was perfect for his purposes. There were three different exits from the building and he could be out on the street quickly. Taking one route to his car, he'd be there in four minutes, the second took five. The third route would be strictly emergency because it would leave him on foot for almost ten minutes, too large a margin for error.

The following afternoon he casually walked from the building he would use to the center of the parking lot. The first block was 205 paces and the second to the center of the lot 175 paces. This gave him a distance of 380 paces or approximately 315 yards. He calculated the angle of elevation and estimated 330 yards to the target. He was now ready to complete his plan. That night he took a plain envelope, pasted Gallagher's address on it (using an old letter found in Gallagher's trash) and put in one of the Queen of Spades. He sealed the envelope with tap water and, still wearing his gloves, posted the letter. If conditions were right next Thursday would be the night. He would wear his old blue jeans, a dark sweat shirt, sneakers, and his gloves. He cleaned every part of his equipment, again wearing his gloves. If he had to abandon the rifle it would be untraceable. Until he completed his mission he would touch none of it with his bare hands.

*   *   *

Thursday evening finally arrived. The Hunter left his apartment and headed for the loft. He arrived at 8 P.M. and prepared his firing position. He made a check of the parking area through his telescope. His pulse quickened slightly; Gallagher's car was there. He knew it would be approximately 11 P.M. before he came out. And so he settled down to wait. He observed the traffic. As usual, it was light. The patrol car went by at 9:30 P.M. He knew it would be almost 12 P.M. before it would normally return. Tonight, of course, it would be back within minutes of receiving word that a shooting had taken place.

At 10:45 P.M. he took up his firing position and released the safety. He now watched the front door of the club through his scope. A couple of customers came out and went to the parking lot. He could see them clearly. Excellent. About ten minutes later his vigil was rewarded when he saw Gallagher come out the door. He tracked him as he walked through the parking lot toward his car. He realized he had to wait until that moment when Gallagher would either hesitate for a full second or be completely still, for it would take the bullet almost a second to travel the distance. He took up the slack between finger and trigger, took a deep breath, let a little out and watched. He could hold this position for a minute and a half. Gallagher had taken his key ring out and started to put a key in the door lock. While he paused, looking for the keyhole, the Hunter squeezed the final hair-breadth needed and the rifle bucked. There was a little flash and the noise was partially muffled because of the flash suppressor on the muzzle. In a split second the rifle had resumed its initial lay on the

53

target. The Hunter saw the top of Gallagher's head split open and the window glass behind him shattered. In slow motion the body crumpled beside the car. The Hunter drew back from his firing position. In one minute he had the rifle returned to its carrying case and was padding lightly to the exit he had chosen. Five minutes later he was heading home in his car.

It took, perhaps, ten minutes before a woman and her companion, walking to their car, discovered the body. Five minutes later the first patrol car arrived and put a call in to homicide. By the time detectives had arrived the Hunter had returned home and had already carefully removed the spent round from the chamber. He had started out with 200 rounds and each had been carefully accounted for—none left lying anywhere. The police completed their initial search for witnesses and clues and allowed the body to be transported.

*   *   *

The next day, when Lieutenant Donelly came on duty, the folder was on his desk. An information copy had been sent to the Organized Crime Task Force because of the victim's background. Donelly noted the name and something nudged his memory, but after a few minutes he shrugged it off. He read the police report and the medical examiner's report. The police report didn't have any surprises; no witnesses and no leads. The Medical Examiner's report indicated that Gallagher had been shot with some type of high velocity round, bits of which had been removed from the head and turned over to ballistics. He had died instantly and there were no other remarkable findings. The ballistics report only indicated it was done with a rifle, most likely .30 caliber, but not enough fragments had been recovered to make positive identification.

On his pad Donelly wrote down some comments:
1. Was this a crime of passion?
2. Was this a crime of revenge?
3. Was this the start of a gang war?

He knew Gallagher was a ladies' man and this was the reason for his first question. In his line of work you automatically made enemies and this led to question number 2. Question number 3 was the one that bothered him. The Task Force should be able to monitor that one and give him information. Item 2 didn't seem to fit because people bent on revenge usually opt for the personal touch: knife, pistol, shotgun—something close range. He made a note for Sergeant Monero to check out items 1 and 2. He'd handle number 3 himself.

*   *   *

At about the same time Donelly was reading his report, Marco Benotti and two of his lieutenants were sitting and listening to a third in another section of town. "We don't know who did it, Mr. Benotti. There hasn't been a rumble around here in months. No outsiders in town. Could it be a jealous husband or something like that? I've put out the word on the streets for any information." He then sat quietly.

After a short silence Benotti finally spoke. "Okay, Archie, it was a good report. Keep after the street angle. We can't allow someone to come in here and burn one of our own people without doing something about it. I want the husband angle also checked out." He then looked at one of the others. "I want you to make sure Gallagher gets the best treatment. Have Damoni's handle the body. That's where Calucci works. We want it known we take care of our own." With that he got up, ending the meeting, for he had other fish to fry. One of the city ward leaders was dropping by later and he wanted to be ready. Maybe they could get some help from the police. It made him smile, a private little joke.

12.

When he came to work two days after Gallagher's death, Calucci got the word that the body would be released from the morgue and that they could start burial preparations. He didn't know why, but he felt a little uneasy, and he shrugged it off as a natural reluctance to work on a friend. Since Gallagher had no family in the area (a sister indicated she would not attend) the Organization would pick up the tab for the funeral. "Maybe that's it," Calucci thought. "If I go, it's the same way I'll go; nobody caring, no family, and no real friends." The uneasy feeling returned.

While Calucci was preparing to pick up the body, Lieutenant Donelly and Sergeant Monero were at Gallagher's apartment looking for clues. They had pretty well turned the place over but thus far hadn't found anything of value. It was a dead end. Donelly looked up from the dresser drawer as he slammed it shut and said to Monero, "You about finished? The place looks clean to me."

Vince answered, "As soon as I finish with this waste basket. Looks like old junk." He held up a crumpled Queen of Spades and asked Donelly, "Did you find a deck of cards anywhere?"

Donelly answered, "No. What did you find?" He took the card, looked at it, and threw it back into the trash. "That's probably the reason he threw it away; the rest of the deck is gone." With that they locked the apartment and left.

*   *   *

The Hunter started stalking his next quarry. He followed Calucci to work for a couple of days, looking for a pattern. On the third day he was rewarded when Calucci went to the large house in the suburbs. So he *was* a member. Somehow it made the Hunter feel better knowing for sure he was a member of the Organization. He didn't stay long at Benotti's and returned to the funeral home.

Unlike Gallagher, Calucci was quite a ladies' man. He seldom stayed home in the evening and was with a different

56

girl almost every night. After three weeks Calucci's pattern finally emerged. At least twice a week he took the same girl out, and even though the times varied, the place was consistent. It would do. It was in the suburbs and this should reduce witnesses or other interference. Now he had to check the area out for proper positioning. He noted that after the girl got out of the car Calucci always sat there for perhaps five minutes or so making sure his date was all right. He did this for all his girls. This was excellent, for Jason only needed him to hold still for a few seconds.

The next morning he toured the area. He noted main streets and cross streets, access to and from the girl's home. Approximately one block away he found a house for sale. He looked at the angle. "It might work," he thought. That night, a Saturday, Calucci picked up his date on schedule. The Hunter, instead of following them, parked his car in front of her home and walked down the street. After making sure no one was watching he slipped to the rear of the house that was for sale. In a couple of minutes he was inside.

He moved quickly through the house into the front room. Just as he suspected, the house projected a few feet beyond its neighbors. His margin for anonymity would be reduced but it would be early morning and he should be able to get away without being seen. He left from the rear door and cut through the yard behind to the next street. Perfect. Once past this house he cut through another yard where his car would be parked on a main artery into the city. He checked his watch; two minutes from the house to his car. Anyone hearing the shot and waking up wouldn't see him before he got out of the neighborhood. He walked around the block again. The distance from the house to his car was 150 yards. It would be like shooting fish in a barrel. He moved his car to the proposed parking area and covered his route back to the empty house. If worse came to worse he could ditch the rifle and catch a bus, leaving his car to be picked up after the excitement died down.

While he was mulling this over, Calucci and his girl returned and went into the house. The Hunter observed all this through his binoculars. The scene was perfect. There was a street light right near the house that gave him plenty of light. After an hour Calucci came out. As usual he sat in his car and the Hunter watched him through the binoculars. He was satisfied. Next Saturday could be the date. That night, when he returned to his apartment he mailed the second letter.

*   *   *

On Tuesday Calucci received the card in the mail. He looked at it for some minutes but it meant nothing to him. Maybe it's a practical joke. He'd call Joe Peroni later, maybe he'd know. He stuck the card back into the envelope and tossed it into a dresser drawer. He had to get back to work. That afternoon he called Joe but he could throw no light on the mysterious "letter." Tony shrugged it off; someone is laughing at him. He'd better not catch him. By the end of the week he had forgotten about it.

Saturday night the Hunter again made his preparations carefully. He dressed in dark clothing. Putting on his gloves he cleaned and oiled his weapon. When it was in its carrying case it attracted little attention, no more than a person carrying a trombone or similar instrument. He drove to his destination cautiously and parked his car, moved over his access route to the empty house, and rechecked his emergency exit and route. He wouldn't need it, but it never hurt to be ready. He returned to the house and snuffed out his last cigarette until the job was done. He didn't want to leave the odor of smoke behind.

As the time passed lights in the homes nearby began to flicker out as people went to bed. By 11:30 P.M. almost all houses were dark, the area quiet except for an occasional passing car. Around 1:00 A.M. all lights were out. But as the neighborhood settled in for the night, the Hunter came quickly alert. A car was approaching. It was him. Jason rapidly assumed his firing position (he would fire from the middle of the room for this would reduce muzzle flash to almost nothing and should help reduce the sound of the round going off). It was late and he was fairly sure Calucci wouldn't go inside tonight. He was right. The girl got out of the car and walked into the house.

The Hunter released his safety and peered into his scope. He could see Calucci clearly, watching the house. When he turned his head and faced to the front again, he would fire. He took up the slack as Calucci turned to start his car. The rifle bucked and by the time it returned on target Calucci was dead. The bullet passed through the windshield and struck Calucci just above the upper lip, passing through his head, removing the rear portion, and passing out the rear window. Inside the room the noise had been fairly loud; outside it had sounded like a backfire. The Hunter replaced his weapon in its case, walked out the rear door and across his planned route. Minutes after he fired, he was starting his car to return to his apartment.

*   *   *

Sometime later, as she was finishing her preparations for bed, Betty Jean glanced casually out her front window. That's strange, she thought. Tony's car is still there. Maybe I should invite him in, he's been so persistent. She pulled on her housecoat and went out to the car. What she saw sent her into hysterics. It wasn't pretty. Within minutes half the neighborhood was there rubber-necking. The police and ambulance arrived and the clean-up started. The only thing anyone could remember was a man waking up and hearing what he thought was a car backfiring. Betty Jean knew absolutely nothing. A wrecker showed up to tow the car to the police impounding lot.

*   *   *

When Lieutenant Donelly entered his office the next morning he was greeted by Sergeant Monero. "Looks like we got another of those high-powered jobs." Donelly looked at him for a few seconds, opened the folder, and started reading. The medical examiner and ballistics had nothing new to report. They hadn't found the bullet, only a few fragments, the theory being that the round had disappeared into limbo once it passed through the rear window of the car.

Donelly looked up at Vince and said, "We can now forget about a crime of passion. I want you to concentrate on revenge. Run a computer check on any crimes we believe they were both involved in. There has to be a connection somewhere. I'll make an appointment with Mr. Bonotti to see if we can rule out gangland. Someone could be trying to muscle in. Captain Eddy of the Task Force says he hasn't heard a word about it, but it may just be getting started. I also want to check out Calucci's apartment. Make sure it's sealed until we can get there."

As he left to comply, Vince thought the Lieutenant was really getting worked up. What was another hood more or less? Maybe they'd get together and bump each other off. That would be nice.

About an hour later Monero came back with the computer matchups. One was quite long, the second a little shorter. He explained to Donelly: "I made two lists, the first is every case involving the rifle as a weapon and the second are cases where the two were suspected as being involved. The rifle list has 28 cases, if you exclude muggings and assaults, which would make the list too long to handle."

Donelly grunted his understanding and said, "I'm not even sure we're on the right track. I'm trying to cover all angles of this. It has to be either the start of a gang war, a vendetta, gang war or a revenge action—a vendetta. I've got the keys for Calucci's apartment. Let's go over and take a look." On the way they got a call that Calucci's brother wanted to know when they'd release the body and Donelly told the dispatcher anytime the medical examiner was finished. A few minutes later they pulled up in front of Calucci's apartment house.

They began a meticulous search of the apartment, going from room to room together, starting with the living room.

They didn't really know what they were looking for, though they'd know when they found it. Vince turned up a pistol in the kitchen (a switchblade had been on the body), and they came across an old-fashioned, wooden handled ice pick. The two weapons they tagged and bagged; they would deliver them to the lab when they returned to headquarters.

As Donelly started through the dresser he came upon the envelope with the card in it. The lights started flashing and gongs went off in his head—it shouted clue! He didn't know the significance of the card only that it had showed up twice in the same investigation. Too much for mere coincidence. He knew that in the old days the mobs were accustomed to sending calling cards to each other during gang wars. So far it also meant the sniper or snipers were being very selective in their targets. The ice pick also would prove important because of the murder of Barker a few months earlier. That had been a weird one. What a way to go, with an ice pick in the ear. He just hoped some of the things they were picking up would shed some light on the case.

He called Vince over and added the card to the pile going to the lab. He was very certain now that they were dealing with either a vendetta or simple revenge as a motive. The old case files gained in importance right away; also a talk with Benotti. It would have to wait until tomorrow though, for this evening he had to report to the Chief of Detectives on the status of his cases. On the way back to headquarters he told Vince to check on ice picks as the modus operandi.

*　　　　*　　　　*

While Donelly and Monero had been searching Calucci's apartment, a meeting was taking place across town. This one was getting a little noisy and Benotti finally shouted, "Shut up all of you! Yelling at each other is getting us nowhere. We have to think this out. I've been assured by the people back east there is no attempt to try and make us look bad."

Benotti had been taking notes on a piece of paper since the meeting had begun. He now replaced his pen with a fresh cigar which he used to punctuate each word. The people around the table knew the habit well. When he started with the cigar bit it meant he was really upset. One of the jokes going around was that it made him feel like one of the old time big shots. The habit had started after he'd seen it in an old gangster movie in his younger days. He very seldom smoked one, only chewed the end until he threw it away and started on another. There was more than one who thought it made him look ridiculous, though no one dared tell him so.

Aaron Greenblatt spoke up immediately. "This is a professional hit, Marco. If the people back east are with us, who then?" He sat glaring at his companions.

Benotti now started ticking off assignments. "Aaron, I want you to concentrate on what the police are doing, see if you can find out any leads they've developed." He turned to Enrico Damoni and said, "I want all your people to canvass the city. I want to know what they're saying on the street." To the third he ordered, "I want you to quietly start a check from this end up. I don't think anyone is trying to move in but I want to be sure."

The buzzer on his intercom rang. It was his secretary calling from her outside office. "Mr. Peroni is here and wants to see you at once. He says he has something that might be connected with the Tony Calucci affair." Benotti looked at the other three. Each nodded assent. He depressed the button. "Send him in." A moment later Joe Peroni stood in front of important company.

He started at once. "Mr. Benotti, you asked me to remember anything I could about my last meeting with Tony. The reason I didn't think of it before was that actually my last contact was by phone. I didn't make any connection until this morning. A few days before they got hit both Mike and Tony asked me the same question but in different ways. Both wanted to know if in our background we had placed any significance on the Queen of Spades. I didn't know of anything and told them so. Mike had thought it was a practical joke."

Everyone at the table looked at each other. There was much negative head shaking. The possibility of this being in the distant past would have to be checked out but none of the people in the room knew anything about it. Benotti asked Joe, "Did they tell you why they wanted to know this?"

Joe answered, "Tony said nothing about it and Mike mumbled something about a practical joke and a letter in his mail box."

Benotti looked around the room again and this time he spoke to the room at large. "So, a letter comes through the mail and a few days later Mike is dead. Not long after, Tony is ambushed and both have mentioned the Queen of Spades. As of now the Queen of Spades means nothing but I want it checked. Someone with a calling card, if that's what it is, it spells out vendetta. We have to stop it at once." He looked around the table, black piercing eyes flashing, challenging anyone to dispute his assessment of the situation. There was none. "Okay, let's concentrate on this vendetta angle. I want to know if anyone has a real grudge against us. If it is a vendetta then we'll find the family responsible and they'll wish they were never born." With that he waved his cigar, indicating that the meeting was over.

*   *   *

Roberts sat in a small bar on the fringe of the middle-class area of the city sipping a beer. He had been coming in here perhaps once a week since returning to the city. It was a good location for his purposes; there was a smattering of clientele from both areas, the middle-class of suburbia and the inner city. It was a place to pick up useful information from time to time. It was here he first heard the word was out that the Organization wanted to know of any newcomers in the town. At first he had been a little nervous

63

but settled down immediately. It was evident the bartender no longer considered him an outsider or he wouldn't have said anything to him. So far his cover was working, but he would have to check out the neighborhood where he lived as well. He didn't want anyone looking into his activities.

After a decent interval he left the bar and returned to his apartment. He had to do some thinking and he needed a clear head and time. He fixed himself a sandwich and sat down to eat it and ponder his situation. He was halfway home. He had known when he started that this would be the time period when he would be in the most danger. Fortunately for him, street information traveled down as well as up. He now had his warning; he had to move carefully. From the newspapers and television news he was aware that the police were after the mysterious rifleman. So far they were only speculating on the reason for the shootings. There had been no mention of the Queens. Perhaps they didn't know about them or they knew and like old television programs this was a clue they were holding back. He opted for the latter. He knew Lieutenant Donelly and he knew he was a very competent and perceptive policeman. After Peroni he would change his base of operation. It paid to be meticulously careful. He went to bed, promising himself that tomorrow he would think it through some more.

The next morning he left his apartment, as he had been doing for weeks, ostensibly to go to work. There had only been two persons who had asked but he told them he sold grinding equipment and traveled quite a bit. This had appeared to satisfy the manager but you never knew for sure. There had been no further questions. He drove out into the country for he had a lot of time to kill before evening. He also had to plan his next move. Peroni was the target, but he didn't want to move too quickly. He also didn't want to waste time either, since there was always a chance a loose word or action would trigger the uncovering of his identity.

That evening he walked into a tiny bar and restaurant.

He had been coming in occasionally to eat here. He usually entered quietly, had a couple of drinks at the bar and then ate. He had formed the usual customer/bartender friendship—extremely casual, but friendly. They talked of baseball, other sports news, and women. Sometimes other customers would join in but Roberts always remained a little separate, a little remote from any close relationship with anyone. Tonight, though, was somewhat different, for he felt the need to unwind. He looked around the dimly lit lounge and his gaze slowly came to rest on a woman sitting quietly at a table near the front of the lounge.

She was very attractive, with an indefinable aura of femininity. It had been a long time since he'd approached a strange woman for the sole purpose of getting better acquainted. He'd seen her before and recalled that she had an easy, self-assured walk when moving from one place to another. In some ways she appeared to be almost out of place here. She should be dining in a somewhat classier place. He remembered watching her rebuff other approaches on more than one occasion and wondered if he would fare any better. Well, nothing ventured, nothing gained, so they say.

He also realized he'd seen her watching him. When this happened before he had shrugged it off because he didn't want to be distracted. Tonight he felt different. He called the waitress over and told her to take the lady a drink. He watched, and when the drink was delivered, gave a little salute. The lady acknowledged the gesture and accepted the drink. Roberts waited a few moments and walked over to the table, drink in hand. "Mind if I sit down?" he asked.

"Not at all," she replied. "I want to thank you for the drink."

Roberts answered, "It's my pleasure. I've noticed you in here before and finally got up the nerve to meet you. My name is Don."

"Mine's Irene," she smiled. "I've noticed you before also and was hoping one day you might notice me."

Don laughed. "You don't have to worry about that. A woman like you would attract men like bees to honey. You're very beautiful."

She had a low, seductive voice that sent chills up his spine. He could tell it wasn't an affectation, but her normal tone. He liked her immediately. It had been a long time since he had been with a woman.

Now that he was next to her he could see she had light brown hair and liquid blue eyes. About 5 feet 6 inches and slender, with a shapely bosom, he would guess her age somewhere in the mid-thirties. Very attractive indeed, she was, and it was obvious she liked him. She snapped him from his inner thoughts.

"Have you been here long? In the city I mean. It seems I've been here most of my life." Then the inevitable question. "Are you married?"

Don thought for a moment, a quick rush of remorse passing through his mind but answered, "No, I was, but it's been over for some time. I came here about a year ago; my company transferred me." He could see the relief on her face. "Have dinner with me tonight?"

She nodded. He paid the bill and they left. He had a special place in mind. They drove to Benotti's supper club. While they dined Don continually looked around to get the feel of the place. It was an excellent meal and over much too soon. He and Irene had been engaged in conversations in which they each sought out mutual interests. He knew she would make up her mind about him during this time.

It had been small talk; people trying to feel each other out. He didn't want the evening to end and he tried to convey to her his desire to continue the relationship. He definitely didn't want her to feel this was just a causal pickup; that she was simply an object of his sexual desire. It was more than that, though he lusted for her as well. Like an awkward schoolboy, groping about for the right thing to say to her, nonetheless, he felt incredibly comforted by her company.

Irene, too, had been making her own evaluations. He was quite handsome and obviously well educated. Yet his attraction was in some strange way completely inexplicable to her. She sensed his desire, which she reciprocated, but also his shyness, which served to excite her all the more. As time wore on she realized that she would make the first move.

As they left the club she turned to him and said, "Would you like to spend the night with me?"

She could see the look of relief and pleasure in his face as he said, "Yes, I would . . . I'll follow you in my car."

With that they drove through the city to a residential section where she pulled up in front of a small bungalow. He parked his car and joined her. Hand in hand they walked to the front door. It was cozy and warmly lit inside. She hung up her coat, came up to him and they embraced. He could feel the promise in her body and his pulse quickened. "Do you want a drink?" she asked. "I do. Fix one for me while I go attend to some private business. Everything you need is in the kitchen." She turned toward the bedroom as he headed for the kitchen and started looking through cupboards and the refrigerator.

When he came back into the living room she was already there, having changed into a house coat. He handed her a scotch and soda and lit a cigarette. She turned on the radio. It had been a long time for him and the biological urge was becoming overpowering. He could tell through her silken robe that she was everything he had imagined. They sat together in the dim light listening to music, embraced again, and this time he felt her hand on his thigh, gently caressing. He slipped his hand inside her robe and ever so tentatively began to fondle her breasts until he could feel her stir with pleasure. Without a word they went into the bedroom.

*   *   *

The next morning, over coffee, he told her he had to leave town but would call her as soon as he returned. She was a little disappointed but accepted his explanation graciously. She looked even more appealing this morning than she had the night before, if that was possible, but he had work to do.

Driving home, he felt peculiarly exhilarated and yet relaxed. He caught a glimpse of himself smiling in his rearview mirror and marvelled at the contradictions within himself as he set out, once more, upon his deadly task.

13.

On Monday he drove by Peroni's home. He sat in his car a block away and watched and waited. About 10 A.M. Peroni came out and drove away. The Hunter followed, staying a block behind. Peroni drove to a small office in the suburbs on the west side of the city. It was in a small shopping center with numerous little shops, fairly new and well attended by the local population. Jason was able to sit in the lot without attracting attention. Peroni would be a little difficult. He was a family man and would have to be dealt with during the day, so he would have to extremely careful about witnesses.

He followed Peroni for two weeks. Every Friday he picked up another man and they followed a standard route. It was evident the passenger was a bag man. This was the only routine the Hunter had been able to discover. It would be risky. The bag man usually took about five minutes at each stop. They never left the city so there would be traffic to contend with. Whatever he decided his escape route would be the overriding factor in any plan. He had made the decision that it must be done on Friday, but he had yet to find the right location.

That evening he called Irene. He told her he was back and wanted to see her. She told him to come over about 8 P.M.

When he arrived at her home it was evident she didn't want to go anywhere. She offered him a cup of coffee and talked about her job. She was employed as an office manager for a construction firm downtown and it was obvious she enjoyed her work. It had been months since he'd sat and listened to a woman talk about her life. He thought of his wife and felt a pang of remorse. Yet he knew that it was madness to live on memories. Irene asked him about his trip and he said it had been very successful. As a matter of fact they would celebrate a little the following night. She was happy and that made Don feel good.

She came over to pour him more coffee and as she did so he ran his hand up the back of her thigh under her skirt and gently rubbed. He heard her sigh and put the pot down. She turned to him. He could feel the soft skin of her buttocks under his hand. It was a long, drawn-out kiss and he was intoxicated with the smell of her.

He pulled her to his lap, opened her blouse, and ran his hand over her breast. The nipple was firm and hard. She moaned as he took a nipple in his mouth, running his tongue over it. As she reached down for him he could feel himself start to lose control. He couldn't fathom this animal attraction they had for each other. It was going to be a wonderful weekend.

*   *   *

During the week, while the Hunter had been following Peroni, Lieutenant Donelly and Sergeant Monero had also been busy. The computer printouts had been too bulky, too much information to sort through. They made it a routine that, for at least an hour each day, they would sift through these reports trying to find the connection, if any, that would give them a point of departure. The pistol found in Calucci's apartment had been registered and never involved in any crime. The ice pick, while still going through analysis, offered nothing conclusive to connect it with any crime.

Monero reported that the street people knew nothing, though rumor was that someone was trying to muscle in. Some thought the "Black Mafia" were trying to control the drug traffic. Others on the street thought it was a vendetta because a family had been cut out of a business arrangement. Lieutenant Donelly looked and listened to Monero. This was a hodge-podge of speculation that led nowhere. The people on the street were guessing. He said to Monero, "I made an appointment to see Benotti. I probably won't learn anything, but I have to touch all bases."

"When you do see Benotti, want me to come along for moral support?"

70

"No, Vince, I'll go alone. I'm to meet him tomorrow morning, Thurday, at 9:30 A.M. I don't know yet if I'll tell him about the Queen of Spades or not. I'll wait and see if he brings it up." With that he and Vince opened another case pertaining to a husband and wife murder. That one, at least, looked pretty much open-and-shut.

*   *   *

On Thursday morning Donelly was ushered into Marco Benotti's office. It wasn't the first time he'd been there and the plushness of the surroundings didn't impress him one iota. Marco stood up behind his desk and indicated a seat directly in front of him. Donelly looked him over. He hadn't changed much. He ran the dossier over in his head: 5 feet 10 inches, 170 pounds, 53 years old, dark hair, brown eyes, rather handsome face but marred by a small scar running from the left eye to his left ear, a result of a fight while still in high school. He had numerous arrests but no convictions. Very intelligent, a smooth operator, and extremely dangerous. To Benotti he said, "Good morning, Benotti, I'm sure you know why I'm here."

Sitting down, Benotti didn't answer directly, but said, "Can I offer you coffee, Lieutenant? I was just about to have some before you came in." Donelly indicated he wanted none and Marco nodded to the secretary who left them alone. He then answered Donelly's question. "No, Lieutenant, I can't imagine why you're here but if I can help I'll be glad to do so." He then sat back in his chair, hooded eyes watching.

Donelly came right to the point. "It looks like two of your soldiers have bitten the dust but you don't look too concerned. Did you have it done and that's the reason you don't care?"

Benotti didn't move a muscle. "I don't have soldiers. I'm a respectable businessman and if you're not careful I'll have City Hall fall on you."

Donelly smiled. "Threats, yet. Did I strike a nerve?"

"No you didn't, I just don't like the implication. A couple

71

of my acquaintances have had unfortunate accidents but I know nothing about it. I was hoping the police could tell me something."

Donelly looked at him and thought, "How much should I tell him; what's the best approach?" Aloud, he said, "I came here for information. Right now we see three possibilities: one, vendetta, two, gang war, and the third, internal removal. I was hoping you'd eliminate one of the reasons so we could concentrate on the other two."

Benotti mulled that over for a moment and answered, "Donelly, I can assure you the third alternative can be eliminated, the second I won't comment on, but the first is interesting. Why include it?"

Donelly replied, hunching forward in his chair. "Let's stop fencing. Of all the people you have, the pushers, collectors, the pimps, the whores, someone is only hitting your enforcers. That's why we've included number one." He then sat back, satisfied that he could tell from Benotti's expression he'd said something the Master hadn't considered. As a matter of fact, the thought had only occurred to him moments before; another little piece of knowledge rippling through his subconscious and finally coming out into the open.

Benotti recovered quickly, uneasy of the momentary lapse in his composure. "That's interesting conjecture, Lieutenant, but it means nothing to me because I don't know what you're talking about. I don't see where this is getting us anywhere and I have a business to run."

Donelly heaved himself up from the chair and turned to leave. Just as he got to the door he turned. "I would appreciate it that if you get any ideas, you'd let me know. I feel this one will turn out to be a case of mutual interest." With that he departed. As he walked to his car he felt he had been quite successful, more by Benotti's reaction than anything Benotti had said. He was certain now it was either a vendetta or revenge of some type. Benotti had really been surprised when he singled out the two enforcers by job

72

rather than name. Neither had mentioned the cards, but Donelly felt in his bones that Benotti knew about them. Still, as he returned to headquarters he realized that if something concrete didn't turn up soon, it looked as if these cases would end up in the unsolved category.

*   *   *

The Hunter was sitting in his car observing traffic near an expressway ramp. He had been here approximately an hour. For a week he'd been driving the collection route, noting times and distances. Peroni and his bag man had, so far, always traveled the same route and were pretty much on time. Their routine never varied more than fifteen minutes and that would have to do. If he couldn't find a suitable place he'd have to get him at home though he didn't want to do that unless it became absolutely necessary. After watching the traffic flow he decided that this location was too risky. Once on the expressway he'd be committed to a direction and distance he didn't feel was justified. This was the third spot he had rejected because of the danger inherent in his withdrawal route. While this site would have been perfect for the kill itself, he knew that everything had to be right or he wouldn't do the job.

He drove to the next spot and parked his car near the pick up point. It was on the fringe of the downtown business district. Nowhere Peroni could park; he always used a loading zone space. He slowly walked up and down the street going up one side and down the other. The road was fairly open without much traffic, and was flanked by a number of small businesses with tight parking arrangements. All of them seemed prosperous. As he walked along the near side of the street he noticed most of the buildings on the other side were of one story construction, except the last one on the block which was two stories high. What interested him the most, though, was that the buildings a block away were five or more stories high. But before he checked out those buildings he would look at access routes.

He walked back to his car and carefully drove around the area. The taller buildings along the next block appeared to be primarily warehouses. Most had truck bays and unloading docks. They didn't appear to be overly busy, though the street itself looked crowded. He drove to the next cross street. This looked better. The only problem, as he saw it, was that he'd be on foot for at least a block and a half. Would he be conspicuous? He didn't think so. There were people walking along carrying all types of boxes and parcels. He would have to come back to this location later on in order to get inside the center building. He drove two more blocks to a main artery going across town. He still had a couple of other drops to check out. He would examine them all out before deciding. There was no hurry and he wanted to make sure.

That evening he returned to the location, parking his car on the next cross street. He walked along in front of the warehouses, especially eyeing the one in the center. As far as he could tell, after a few hours of observation, there was only one watchman for all three buildings. In two hours he had seen no prowl cars. The watchman left the first building and headed for the second. Apparently he had to check each one hourly. The Hunter walked around the corner and entered the alley behind the buildings. At last he found what he was looking for; an open window on the second floor, only partially open but it meant that any alarm system would be inoperative. He climbed on a commercial trash container and within seconds was standing inside. He checked the window from the inside. No alarm. He moved to the stairs, climbed to the top floor and went to the rear of the building. He silently raised a window and gazed out over the alley and the roof tops of the next row of buildings. Beautiful. He could see the far side of the next street clearly. Even at this late hour there were a few cars parked along the curb. He could see the loading zone which Peroni used. So far, so good. How to get in while the people were working, though, and more important, how to get out? He checked his watch. The watchman would be in

74

the third building. He went back out the window, lowering it before he dropped to the alley. He returned to his car and drove home. It was only then that he removed his gloves.

The next morning wearing work coveralls and a baseball cap he walked to the warehouse. He was carrying a suitcase with only his binoculars inside and a tag on the outside. He walked through the door. There was no one there. He could hear forklifts working in the background which was a good sign. He walked to the stairs and climbed to the fifth floor. There was no one working here, either. Apparently every one was employed on the first two floors, the upper stories being used for long term storage. This fit into his plans perfectly and he sat down by the rear window to wait and watch. He knew Peroni and the bag man would be in the vicinity between 2:30 P.M. and 3:30 P.M. When the time for action came he observed the street scene in the area of the hit through his binoculars. During this dress rehearsal it all looked normal. No apparent problems. He picked up his suitcase and headed for the front door. Before exiting he waved to a man holding a clipboard who waved back. Once out in the street he got in his car and drove home. The next day was Friday. He repeated the procedure of the day before. This time he saw the dispatcher on the way in but was not challenged. Peroni and the bag man arrived at 2:45 P.M. and Peroni parked right where he always did in the loading zone. The Hunter had a perfect view. With the binoculars he could see him clearly sitting in the car. There would be certain amount of risk this time but he felt confident that he could pull it off. He heard the muffled sounds of street traffic and the hum of fork lifts; no one should hear anything over this noise. He smiled. It was a long shot, about 350 yards, but he felt good about his chances. That night, after he arrived home, he prepared the third card and mailed it.

*　　　　　*　　　　　*

On Monday Joe Peroni picked up his mail at the insurance agency. When he opened the letter with the card inside his mouth went dry. He felt a tightness in his chest

75

and his face drained of all color. The salesman at the next desk jumped up. "Are you okay, Joe? You look sick." Peroni looked at him a moment and said he was all right, an upset stomach. He thought to himself, "I can't panic, I have to remain cool, I have to see Benotti. He'll know what to do." He called Benotti who told him to come over as soon as he could. Joe told his companions he was going to get some stomach acid pills, he'd be back later. He went to the door but hesitated. He looked over the parking lot carefully but could see nothing, for the Hunter had set up his blind elsewhere.

When he arrived at Benotti's office there were two of his lieutenants already present. Peroni said nothing, only handing the card to Benotti. Benotti picked up the Queen with reluctance, a strange feeling coming over him. He had heard stories of the old days when vendettas among the families were a commonplace event. The custom had practically died out here in America. It was just a plain everyday card, one you could buy in any store. Why did it affect him so? He passed it around without comment, each man holding it only with finger tips as if it were contaminated. He then returned it to Joe. After all, it was his.

He then said, to the room at large, though obliquely directing his comment to Joe, "We know this is not to be considered lightly. You did good, Joe, coming straight to us. We must plan some protection for you and try to find out who is sending these cards." He looked around for comment from the others. After a pause—with no one volunteering to speak—he continued. "We know someone has declared war. I want pressure put on the street people. Someone has to know something. I want Joe provided with protection 24 hours a day. We have to stop this. We can't let people think they can attack our people and get away with it. Joe, I don't want you to go anywhere alone again until we get this resolved." He turned to one lieutenant. "Make the necessary arrangements; I want his house guarded and I want him guarded no matter how long it takes." To Joe he said, "I want your cooperation in this. Don't talk to anyone. Don't worry your wife. We'll take care of you. Now wait outside until we round up a couple of boys to go with you."

The rest of the week Joe moved in a sort of daze. He wouldn't tell his wife what was wrong and this led to a couple of small family spats. He was tense, the least little occurrence setting him off. Always being followed around didn't help any either. The Organization could find no reason for the threats. It was unreal. By Thursday he was starting to relax a little. Nothing had happened and he felt a little better. Still tense and watchful, his immediate fear had begun to wane. Tomorrow was time for the pick-ups. At first he thought of not going, but decided finally that he wasn't going to be buffaloed. What the hell, there'd be an extra man along in case of trouble. Besides, he was more worried when he was home alone.

*   *   *

Friday morning dawned bright and beautiful for the Hunter. Perfect weather. He made his preparations carefully, dressing in a conservative suit. Coat and tie always allayed suspicions if stopped or questioned. The jacket, though, he carefully folded; he would only need it later. Over his street clothes he pulled on a pair of coveralls and put on the baseball cap. He had put the tag from the suitcase onto his rifle carrying case. He stopped at a cafe and had a good breakfast; it would be a long day and he wouldn't get another chance to eat. He then drove to the location and parked in his preplanned spot. It was about 11 A.M. He walked to the warehouse and entered. There was no one at the door. He could hear the forklifts and the normal storage activity. Good. He went up to his observation spot on the fifth floor and prepared his firing position a few feet from the window. He used the "No Parking—Loading Zone" sign to sight on. He had a good, comfortable, prone position and a perfect view. He then sat down to wait. He had to relax as much as possible. How many times had he done this, sat for hours, sometimes without moving, waiting for a target to appear? This was no different. He had learned patience well.

77

For Joe and his companions all had gone well. It was a pleasant day for a drive and they had enjoyed themselves. Joe had almost forgotten the reason for Angelo being with them. In a couple of hours he'd be home watching television. He felt good; with every passing day he felt more at ease. They had passed an armored car and had a laugh. Who needed to be cooped up like that to haul money around? No one ever bothered them. Who would dare?

They only had a couple of more stops. Joe looked at his watch. 2:50 P.M. Right on schedule. He slipped into his usual parking spot and cut the engine. The collector got out and walked back to the store. Joe twisted in his seat while he and Angelo continued their conversation about baseball.

*   *   *

The Hunter had come to alert status around 2:30 PM. He had walked around a little bit to relax all his muscles and then rechecked his equipment. He could hear the people working below, there couldn't be over ten, mostly operating equipment that created quite a din. He looked out over the roof tops to the street below. Normal activity. He lay on the crates and worked a round into the chamber. Engaging the safety, he next tightened his sling and sighted in on the sign below. As he was doing this the sedan pulled in and parked. His pulse quickened slightly. He brought the rifle to bear on Peroni. It was him. He saw him turn in the seat to face the rear. He moved the scope to have his own look. There was an extra man today. No matter.

He released the safety and settled into a firing position. The scope gently came to rest on the back of Peroni's head. The cross hairs covered the base of his skull where the spinal cord and head met. He took a deep breath, released some air, and took up the slack. His body and rifle fused for this moment. Slowly he squeezed the trigger. The rifle bucked and he got that good recoil feeling in his shoulder. The rifle settled on target and he saw Peroni slump. He felt good. He quickly replaced the rifle in the case and hurried downstairs. As he walked out the front door he saw or met

78

no one. He walked to his car and drove off. About a mile away he entered the parking lot of a shopping center and parked. He removed his coveralls, put on his suit coat, straightened his hair and threw the coveralls and cap into a trash container. Looking around once more, he then drove to his apartment.

*   *   *

One moment Angelo Conti had been talking with Joe and the next he was dead. It had all happened so quickly he wasn't even sure he had been a witness. Joe was talking about baseball and suddenly his jaw exploded, spewing teeth and blood all over the front seat. The bullet had entered the back of his head and struck the floor of the car, flattening itself like a pancake. Joe's head snapped back and then what was left hung on his chest and rolled from side to side. One arm was still resting on the back of the seat, the other in his lap. Angelo just stared. It was an unbelievable sight. He was just breaking in and hadn't seen anything like this before.

Angelo was a young man in his mid-twenties. Up to this point he had only been on the fringes of the Organization. He'd been involved in a couple of muscle jobs and some minor collection business. A rather shallow personality, his life was being directed by fantasies he had about becoming a big shot. It was already becoming evident he had neither the brains or ability for his aspirations. This was his first assignment of any importance and he had felt sure that if he did a good job there was a chance he might make it as one of the enforcers being selected to replace the two who had died.

He sat for perhaps a half a minute, unable to move or register what had happened. As soon as he did he jumped from the car and prepared to run, but a large crowd had already started assembling.

The bag man came out of the store, took one look and walked away. He couldn't become involved with this; he had to get the receipts away. He could already hear the sirens approaching.

79

14.

The death of Peroni dropped like a bomb. The newspapers and television reporters were having a field day. It was extremely embarrassing for Marco Benotti. All the protection they had provided for Joe was ineffective. He was fit to be tied. He had called an emergency meeting of the Organization. At Police Headquarters Lieutenant Donelly was being called upon to report to all different types of superiors, including the Commissioner himself. Political pressure was being felt by everyone involved. It was as bad as Donelly had seen it in twenty years on the force; you'd think the Governor had got it instead of some hood. The news media was playing up the "unfortunate family man" bit, forgetting to mention what Peroni's line of work had been. Donelly had a headache, an upset stomach, and no leads.

When he and Monero had arrived on the scene there was complete pandemonium. Angelo Conti had tried to get away from the car but was stopped by some angry citizens who thought he had done it. The first police on the scene had become involved in crowd control and chances to identify real witnesses became nil. The car was a mess but it was evident the job had been done with a high powered rifle. While Monero had interrogated possible witnesses Donelly had looked over the scene. His instincts told him the shot had been fired from the warehouse area in the next block. He would check it out. About that time the Commissioner had arrived to add his voice to the babble all around him.

This time they had a witness but he could provide them with no information. All he had seen was Peroni die. He had neither seen nor heard anything except the plop and squishing when the round had struck Peroni. Donelly had been about to release him when a sudden inspiration made him ask, "What were you doing in the back seat? You've never been along before?"

Angelo had looked frightened and blurted out, "I was there to protect Joe." The implication of what he'd said didn't strike him until Donelly's second question.

"Not the bag man. You were along to help Joe. Why?"

"I don't really know. He'd received some kind of threat. Everyone is uptight. I don't know anything more."

Donelly looked at him a few more seconds. So the Organization was getting edgy. But why Peroni? He was primarily a driver. He'd have to check it out. It meant one thing, though. His hunch had been right. Benotti knew about the Queen of Spades. Just then Sergeant Monero came up and handed him Peroni's personal items. In the plastic bag was the envelope with the Queen of Spades in it. Something definite to go on and yet so elusive, he thought.

After they left the murder scene he and Monero drove to the warehouses on the next street. Identifying themselves as police officers, they started a search. They started with the first warehouse and, when finished, proceded to number two. The dispatcher told them that no unauthorized personnel had been in the warehouse. Donelly and Monero checked out the upper floors anyway. On the fifth floor Donelly walked to an open window and looked out. He got one of those eerie, hair-rising-on-the-nape-of-the-neck feelings, as he studied the area. To Monero he said, "I don't know how I know it, but this is it. I want some lab boys up here to go over this place with a fine tooth comb. I want nothing left to chance. Now we talk to our big mouth downstairs who's so sure no one was here. It looks to me like no one's been here in months except for this spot. Notice the dust has been broken through on the floor and those crates have been disturbed."

Monero acknowledged the order but commented, "It could be one of his workers screwing off up here."

Donelly just shook his head and started for the stairs to the first floor. This time Donelly wouldn't accept evasive answers; he was sure he was on the right track. The dispatcher was reacting nervously to his sharp questioning.

81

Donelly said to him, "Look, I'm not trying to get you in trouble. I need to know is there a possibility someone could get in here without you knowing it?"

The dispatcher squirmed but finally answered, "Christ, Lieutenant, I can't be everywhere at once. I have fifteen guys to supervise all over this place. We hire the people by the day and every day they send a different bunch. It's hard to try and identify any one of them. To answer your question, I suppose someone could come in without me seeing them."

"But not on the top floor." It was a statement.

"No, that's what we call permanent storage. It sometimes doesn't move for months or years," answered the dispatcher.

Before leaving, Donelly asked one more question. "Now you're sure there's been no one about lately? No strangers, no people unknown to you?"

The far away look in the dispatcher's eyes told him he'd struck pay dirt. The man answered. "Funny, I didn't think of it before. There was a guy here a few days ago. I had almost forgotten him. He was dressed like all the other people in here and I didn't see him up close. He waved and said 'Hi' to me and I thought he was a day worker. We get some people, as I said before, from a day labor force downtown to supplement our work force so you don't pay too much attention to strangers."

Donelly asked, "Do you remember anything about him, anything at all? It could be important." God, he thought, this guy probably actually saw the sniper.

The dispatcher answered. "Well, as I said, he had on a pair of coveralls similar to ours and a ball cap. I'd guess he was average height, around 5 feet 10 inches to 6 feet. 170 pounds maybe. Not too old. He was carrying a suitcase with one of our tags on it. That's why I didn't pay that much attention."

Donelly asked him, "If he was walking out with one of your tagged cases wouldn't you have to record it?"

"Nah. Each work group has load or unload lists that they

work from. They keep the record of what's coming in and going out on the spot. I just thought this guy was loading a truck outside. I had other things on my mind too. He may have come right back into the warehouse. I wouldn't know."

After a few more questions he and Monero left to return to headquarters. They had garnered more information and now it had to be sifted. This was the really unglamorous part of police work, going through hundreds of bits of information to find that piece that might hold the rest together.

15.

The Hunter sat in his apartment watching the scene unfold on the television screen. This time the shooting had really created an uproar. He watched and listened carefully to every scrap of information. He wanted to be aware of as much of what the police knew as possible. On the news tonight they mentioned for the first time the Queen of Spades. So now it was out. The poor little creep that had been in the car with Peroni had spilled his guts all over the place and the reporters were right there. The lead headline in the paper had been "Who's Declared War?" followed by a lot of conjecture and few facts by an imaginative reporter. He sipped his coffee, cleaned and oiled his weapon and smiled to himself. He now had an important decision to make. Should he go on and try for Benotti or was he satisfied now that he had taken revenge on the actual murderers?

       *   *   *

Benotti had called an emergency meeting of all his lieutenants. Aaron Greenblatt was there, Damoni, Green and Punchello. This would be an important session. He had been on the phone all afternoon to the state capital and the news he had from the "Big Man" was not good. As a matter of fact Benotti was sweating and had a definite harried look about his eyes. He had been told to clean up this local mess or someone would do it for him. When told this his throat had constricted so much that he could hardly answer. It took all his self-control not to panic. This called for some clear thinking. They had to uncover and stop whoever the people were who were doing the killing. Even his own soldiers were getting nervous because they didn't know who would be next.

He called the meeting to order and everyone, for a change, was silent and attentive. There were furtive glances of distrust passing around the table. It was always possible that someone was trying to move up in the Organization.

This was dangerous business but not unheard of and Benotti was well aware of it. To the group he said, "I've been on the phone for hours with the capital. The heat's really on. They want action. Aaron, what do the police know for sure?"

Aaron cleared his throat. He was a tall, reedy man of about fifty. "Lieutenant Donelly is the senior officer on the case. He's also getting a lot of heat. My contact says he'd settled on revenge or vendetta, leaning more to the revenge motive. He's been running computer match-ups like crazy trying to find a key. If he finds one I'll know it as soon as he does. The only witness to anything so far is Angelo. We finally got to him and told him to shut his stupid mouth before he does more damage. Peroni is the first time they've come up with physical evidence. They know the weapon used is a 30.06 caliber rifle but the bullet was smashed so bad they can't run a ballistics check. They also know about the Queens. They have, actually, from the first. It smells like vendetta to my contact but I don't think Donelly agrees."

Benotti digested that information for a moment or two and then turned to Puchello. "When Donelly and Monero left the scene today they made a stop at a warehouse on the next street. You have people working in there. Find out what they were doing there and the name of anyone they talked to. The gloves are off, so if it takes a little roughing to get information, so be it." Puchello nodded his assent.

Benotti then said to everyone, "It's obvious this guy or group is following our people and picking his spots. I want everyone to start paying attention to who's around them. I want our street people leaned on. This guy has to be holed up somewhere in this city and I want him found. Have them go back as far as a year to see if anyone had been around asking questions. I want some action. Some of the television stations are treating these people like some kind of "Robin Hoods" or avenging angels and it's bringing too much exposure on us. If we don't pay him off soon, every crackpot in the city will start in on us. As soon as any of your people uncover anything report it to me directly. You

85

all have my private number." With that he adjourned the meeting.

*   *   *

Lieutenant Donelly was doing a slow burn. He was pissed because the news media had let the cat out of the bag about the Queens. It was the one positive item he had for identification of the real sniper. Now every nut in town would start turning himself in. He had spent a very uncomfortable hour with the Chief of Detectives and the Commissioner. One positive item came out of the shouting match; he would get a couple of more men. He called to Monero who came into his office.

"Vince, how are we coming on the computer match-ups? I still feel this is a revenge action. The answer has got to be somewhere in the old files. I feel it in my bones."

"Lieutenant, I've narrowed some items down and now, including cases Peroni may have been involved in, there are 18 or 20. It's hard going because some of the people have moved, died, are in stir, or simply disappeared. Our street people aren't coming up with much either."

No, Donelly thought, they're not. Aloud he said to Monero, "We know a couple of things. The Organization is starting to panic a little. That weasel Conti was completely shook up; he was so scared he couldn't spit. We also know this guy is good. The shot on Peroni must have been 300 yards at least. I know before I ask, but did the lab boys find anything in that warehouse?"

"No sir. They went over that entire floor with a fine tooth comb, nothing. The playing cards, envelopes, anything we found that he may have touched is clean as a whistle. It's almost like he was a ghost. Gives you the willies thinking about it. No wonder the troops are shook up. I wouldn't want him after me. By the way, Calucci's ice pick also came back clean."

Donelly didn't say anything for a moment or two, then he finally said to himself, as much as to Monero, "How bad do we really want to find this guy? From a moral standpoint he

86

has to be stopped, but actually who's being hurt? Thugs, thieves, pimps, murderers. The guy is doing us and the city a favor. If this is a vendetta I can't see the connection. Captain Eddy says he knows of none—there hasn't been a rumble of that sort in years. Where or when will it stop? I would like to catch up with this guy before the Organization does. I'm afraid they'll hang him out to dry. I'm not really sure that if I could catch him I would; make him stop maybe, but arrest him? I don't know."

Monero answered at once. "I can sympathize with that, Lieutenant, I feel he's doing us a favor too. Maybe he goes far enough they give him a medal. But there is something I don't like. I feel the Organization is getting our reports as soon as we do. We need to plug that up if we can. Do you have any ideas on who it could be?"

"No," answered Donelly, "but this very case may flush him out in the open. Benotti is really sweating this; his upper echelon can't be too happy with his handling of the situation so I imagine he's getting heat from them as well as his own people. Maybe they'll move too fast in some area and we'll get a line on the informer. All we can do is keep our eyes and ears open."

*   *   *

Don Roberts lay at the pool side in the warm sunshine. He was idly watching Irene swimming. It was a good idea to take her away for a few days. It wasn't for the reason she thought, but he had needed time to think things through. He realized that what he had been doing was morally wrong, but he rationalized that it was all in your viewpoint. An eye for an eye, he had been taught as a young man. He likened himself to the old pioneer who protected his own and killed snakes by himself.

When he started out the moral question had concerned him but he justified his action by telling himself that if no one else would do anything about these vermin, he would. But now his present dilemma: should he go on? The people who had harmed him had been dealt with, but should not the force behind those people also be punished? It was interesting. If he quit now, they would probably never catch him. To go on only involved further risk of discovery and the knowledge that the Organization would hound him to the end of time.

He was shaken from his reverie by Irene who had come from the pool splashing water all over him. The old animal hunger stirred within him as he watched her toweling herself. She finally came and sat beside him. "Happy?" he asked.

"I certainly am," she replied, "I really needed these days to regroup. I haven't had so much fun in years. I wish we could just stay here forever."

He laughed. "Forever is a long time. I have my work to do and you have yours. We both have commitments we have to live with. But it is an interesting thought. I think I'll swim a few laps and then clean up for dinner."

She looked at him for a few moments before answering. "You certainly keep yourself fit. Every morning we've been here you're up at the crack of dawn and running. I know you don't mean to wake me but I always feel it when you're not there." She smiled the most inviting smile. "I'll go in and shower while you're swimming. Don't be long."

"I won't," he answered while getting up. "I'll be finished in 10 or 15 minutes. Keep the water warm for me." With that he dove into the pool. As he swam back and forth he thought, "This is another thing I have to resolve. It's not fair to Irene to be led on, getting her hopes built up for something that can never be." What a mess his life had been turned into by those people. He couldn't—wouldn't—risk endangering her. He cared for her too much. Pulling himself from the pool, he padded towards their room, toweling himself as he walked.

He entered the dim room and at first thought something was wrong. It was so still he could hear his own breathing. He was about to call her name when she stepped from the bathroom. She was completely naked. Christ, but she was beautiful. He caught his breath as he took all of her in, his eyes caressing every contour of her body. He dropped his towel as she started coming toward him. They met in the center of the room and embraced. In a moment she knelt, pulled his swim suit off, took his beautiful erection in her hand and kissed it. Lightning shot through his entire body. She rose to meet his lips, still holding him and tenderly rubbing. He went wild with desire. He carried her to the bed, laid her down, and gently entered her. All he could hear was the sea beating in his ears and her low moans as she pulled him more deeply inside and moved to meet him. Then there was the complete oblivion of passion.

After a while they lay, exhausted, side by side. She was running her hand over his body and he was quietly smoking a cigarette. He was at complete peace with the world. She aroused something in him he had never known was there. The thought of not seeing her gave him pangs of remorse. He would have to think on it. What he did know was that he couldn't allow her to be hurt because of him. She stirred beside him, "A penny for your thoughts." He rolled on his side to face her. "I'm hungry," he answered. "Why don't you take a quick shower and then let's go out for dinner."

"Great," she looked at him for a few seconds and then stretched like a contented cat. "You do know how to satisfy my basic appetites."

16.

Lieutenant Donelly and Sergeant Monero sat in Donelly's office a few weeks after Peroni's shooting. Two other detectives were still going through the old files in the basement that the computer had indicated might be match-ups. It was hot, dusty, tedious work down there and Donelly was glad he didn't have to do it. Once they had them all assembled the matching points would be narrowed until, hopefully, they'd have a manageable number. As time passed and the sniper had not struck again things had quieted down and they were able to pursue their usual investigative routine. It took longer but it frequently provided concrete results. Donelly said to Monero, "We have to screen these old cases and put them in a particular order."

Vince replied, "Right. Have you thought of some classifications to use? The troops in the basement are going stir crazy. They've turned up a huge pile of records."

"Initially we'll break them down into groups," Donelly answered.

"1. Crimes where all three are suspected of being involved.

"2. Crimes where a rifle was involved.

"3. Crimes where vendetta could be the motive.

"4. Organization vs. Organization.

"5. Crimes where revenge is thought to be the motive.

"6. Miscellaneous, anything that doesn't fit anywhere else. I want you to stay on top of this thing. I feel the answer lies in these old cases. We just have to find the key."

"The troops on the street are starting to relax a little," Monero replied, "but my instincts tell me they're making a mistake. I don't think it's over yet."

Donelly, completely alert, looked at Vince as he spoke. "I think it's why we make a good team, Vince. It's almost like ESP. What you said is exactly what was passing through my mind. I'd bet my career we're right."

"You may be doing exactly that. Someone upstairs certainly wants this solved, and I feel it's more than their just wanting us to get our job done," Vince continued. "I've been around this outfit long enough to recognize outside influence."

Donelly agreed. "Yeah. I never remember having been this bugged about any of the rest of our case load. And we've still got Fletcher, from the *News*, on us like a dog after a bone. He smells a story and he's not going to give up. Better keep after those two downstairs and let me know when they have all the files pulled."

*   *   *

Don Roberts sat in the cocktail lounge owned by Benotti. It had been several weeks since his last visit with Irene. He sat passing the time with the bartender. Since he wasn't a regular the small talk centered on baseball and babes. There was a sudden flurry of activity in the background and Don turned to look. Benotti and four others had come in and sat at a table in the rear. Don turned back to the bartender, "Must be some kind of wheel."

The bartender looked at him. "You don't recognize him? That's Marco Benotti."

Don asked idly, "He come here often?"

"Hell, he owns the place," answered the bartender. "He comes in maybe once, twice a week. He conducts a little business here. I understand when he meets with his old cronies, though, he goes to the old place."

Roberts prompted him, "The old place?"

"Yeah, he owns another restaurant on the west side." The bartender paused for a second or two. "It's the place where he got his start years ago,"

"It must be great to be rich," said Roberts, "but I guess I'll never know how it feels." After a few more minutes he got up and left, waving to the bartender as he did so. The bartender was already busy with some new patrons who had just arrived.

As he drove away from the restaurant Roberts remember-

91

ed something Donelly had told him months before: "I don't know who did the actual shooting but I know Benotti ordered it done." The words seared into his mind. So that was his man. He'd recognized him immediately in the club but had played ignorant for the bartender.

He was going after Benotti. It had been a dificult decision for him to make. After his interlude with Irene at the ocean-side he had agonized for days. The thought that finally tipped the scales had been that this man had the power to order life and death over other people, the death of innocents as well as guilty. Even then, guilty by whose standards? The Organization's standards were certainly not the standards and mores of civilized men. And he himself . . . was he guilty? He had read the editorials and letters to the editors and listened to comments on television. Public opinion was 60/40 in favor of the sniper. But it was still his decision and he had made it. He would not play it safe and walk away.

He realized that this time, when he mailed the last card, all hell would break loose. It would be a race: would he get to Benotti, or would the police or the Organization get to him first? He had been observing Benotti for about a week. He would be a tough nut to crack. He didn't have a regular schedule, he never stayed outside for any time longer than necessary to go from car to house. He was never alone, except perhaps in his home. As with the others, he didn't want to do the job at Benotti's home. He needed more background on Benotti. But where would he get it? At last he came upon an idea. He'd try the library for old issues of the local paper. It was a large task but he'd have to try it.

*   *   *

Lieutenant Donelly was sitting at his desk reading case files and making comments for later transcription. It had been another long day and he was exhausted. He had drank so much coffee and smoked so many cigarettes that his mouth and throat felt raw. A bit more to read and he could pack it in. He was completely engrossed and didn't hear

Monero come in, didn't know he was there until he slammed the door. He finally looked up with a question in his eyes.

"Going on our assumption that the Organization murders could be an act of revenge, the junior G-Men downstairs have made some progress."

For a few seconds Donelly just looked at him. The Organization murders were rapidly losing their urgency as time passed. But this pause allowed him to shift gears and get in sync with Monero.

He said to Monero, "Okay, I'm with you. What do they think they have?"

"They're getting things into manageable proportions," then added, "Maybe you'd want to look their files over tomorrow? It's not important yet, no big breakthrough. But if we could define the terms again, it would help. They need a direction to go in if they're going to continue."

Donelly said, "Let's restrict it to the last three years and see if we turn up a manageable number of old cases. If we don't uncover anything we'll take another three years. There's always the possibility someone's been on ice for a few years. We also have to consider the three haven't been together that long either."

*   *   *

The Hunter was in the rolling hills portion of the city's suburbs. He had been driving here almost daily, parking his car and walking around the entire Benotti estate. It was a huge place, covering acres of land. There was a main house the size of a castle, a cottage that appeared to be servant's quarters, a fairly large stable, and a gate house. It was completely surrounded by a stone and brick wall about 8 foot high topped with barbed wire that could be electrified. The Hunter hadn't approached the estate directly; he was still engaged in long range surveillance. The surrounding area was heavily forested except where the trees had been cleared to make spacious lawns and accommodate the majestic homes. The roads were all two lane blacktop or concrete which wended their way along picturesque routes constructed to preserve as much of the aesthetic value as possible. It fitted the Hunter's purposes quite nicely, offering numerous places of concealment for him. He had first driven around the vicinity for familiarization, locating streets and all the entrances into the estate. Once he had all the entrances memorized he drew a map of the layout. He wanted fairly accurate distances to any point on the estate.

One morning he approached the walls of the estate through a cluster of trees that grew almost to the wall. It was near one of the side gates that he was sure went unattended during the day. The main front and rear gates, as he had already observed, were electrically operated and surveillance was by remote control television. He was sure there would be several cameras randomly scattered throughout the estate. As he walked along the wall he studied it foot by foot. The three strands of barbed wire did not appear to be electrified. Suddenly he realized why. There were electrical sensors much like automatic door openers along the top of the wall, just inches above the concrete and the first strand of wire. Anyone breaking the light beam would set off an alarm in the house and pinpoint the intruder's location.

After he satisfied himself that he understood the daytime activity at the estate, he began visiting at night. He had elected a spot near the main entrance where he had excellent concealment and could observe the area from the main gate to the main house. He had to know when and what type of visitors Benotti received. He still didn't want to do the job here but he would if it became necessary. He noted that every evening around 10:00 four dogs were turned loose to roam the grounds. They had no set pattern and could appear anywhere, anytime. Although they were not an insurmountable problem, it could be a complication which might have to be dealt with. Once darkness descended, though, very little activity took place. Once or twice a week Benotti would leave for the city where he'd spend a few hours, but he never returned to the estate late.

He followed Benotti on his infrequent evening trips to town. He was never alone and he never moved on any set schedule. Benotti might go on Wednesday or Thursday this week, Monday and Friday the next and so on. On those occasions the Hunter had followed him in the morning, his driver never took the same route to work. There just didn't seem to be anywhere or anytime he could predetermine where Benotti might be at any given moment. It would get even more difficult after Benotti received his calling card. It would be risky whatever he did, but he was determined to finish what he had started.

He had the definite feeling Donelly was also closing in on him. It was just a matter of time. He also knew from the street people that the Organization was still looking. So far his cover was holding up. After much deliberation he decided to sit tight in his apartment; it was less dangerous to stay where he was than attract attention by moving.

Jason had given up his research project in the library. He had been looking for a pattern of some kind but there just weren't any to be found. Benotti was too unpredictable to pin down.

*   *   *

Aaron Greenblatt's people had also been busy during this period. He had received copies of all reports filed by Lieutenant Donelly's team and was aware of the concept Donelly had about the case. He had also found the reason Donelly and Monero had stopped by the warehouse. His troops had also visited the warehouse and a thoroughly frightened dispatcher had told them all he knew. It was nothing they hadn't already known. They did get from another worker, however, an almost complete description. Added to what they already knew were that the eyes of the man they sought were slate blue and hard as ice.

The description filtered down through the ranks to the street people. They were looking for a white male, about 5 feet, 11 inches tall, age in the early forties, and weight about 170 pounds. He had light brown hair and slate blue eyes. He was a loner and probably moved into the city in the past

95

year. Now the ferrets were really active, for there was a reward for anyone turning this guy over to the Organization. Greed always insures compliance in this type of operation.

While sitting in Benotti's supper club a couple of soldiers were discussing the description. The bartender quit polishing his glasses behind the bar and walked over. It was just possible and he could use the money.

"The guy you were describing, is it important?"

"You bet your sweet ass it's important," one of the soldiers answered. "If you know something you'd better spill your guts."

"Once or twice there's been a guy fitting that description come in here. The only part that doesn't fit is I think he's married."

The other man asked, "What makes you think that? We have to drag everything out of you? If you know something just tell us. We'll decide if it's important."

The bartender, now feeling a little uneasy, hesitated. If he were wrong he was getting a guy into serious trouble. He realized now though he had better tell or he'd be in trouble. Why can't I keep my big mouth shut? "It's been a long time. This guy came in a couple of weeks before Gallagher got it. I didn't see him for weeks and he came in again, stayed a while and left. A few weeks later he came in for dinner with a real looker I assumed was his wife. They've been here twice. He came back alone a couple of weeks ago when Mr. Benotti was here but he didn't stay long. I'm almost sure his name is Don. That's it. That's all I know. Like I said, he's not a loner and he seemed to know the city fairly well so I don't think he's a newcomer."

The soldiers thanked him and another piece of information was fed to Greenblatt. Was it possible he was their man? The wife bit didn't fit, but then this whole deal had been unreal from the start. Aaron paid a visit to the bartender but could learn nothing more. There was something about the way he described this Don character however that made him put the word out on the streets. Sometimes you had to trust your instincts. Of course that particular description could fit several thousand guys in the city.

*   *   *

When Donelly got the word through one of his informants, he was furious. He called in Monero. "The God-damned Organization has a direct pipeline into this bureau. We've got to find it and plug it."

Monero looked pained. "You don't have to yell at me. We've known for months information was leaked, so what's new?"

Donelly just glared, "How in hell can they get complete reports? My informant tells me they've got our complete confidential file, every stinking note or supposition, everything."

"What do you propose to do about it," asked Monero.

"From now on we make only one copy and I'll keep it on my person, in my possession, at all times."

Monero looked skeptical. "They ain't going to like that upstairs."

"Screw 'em. I'm going to wait and see who has the most curiousity, and why, and then I'll feed them only what I want them to know. I have to say one thing. We now have an almost complete description of the sniper and a possible name. Also, there's a possibility he's married, maybe even a family. This means he'll stay put for a while. I want that part concealed from the press if possible. Now, how are you coming on the files?"

Monero brightened a little at this. "I've got it worked out to eight possibles. I have them on my desk if you've got time to look at them."

A few minutes later he had the files laying on his desk. He started through them one by one. Each had the same characteristics:

1. They were Organization hits.
2. All three dead men had been suspects. .

97

3. None were over three years old.

4. Three were ice picks, four were pistol, and one was a shotgun.

He looked at the names: Jackson, Herbert, Mattucci, Popov, Barker, Paolucci, Bendotta and Raines. Was the answer here, as he suspected, or would it be back to square one? To Monero he said, "I want background on everyone involved in each of these cases. If there were witnesses I want the name of their maiden aunt, you got that? I want to know everything about everyone in these files. If the answer's here we'll know it. I want all information you collect locked in your desk. I want you to make sure nothing leaks out."

"Okay, Lieutenant, I'll start on it right away," answered Monero. "Any idea what we're looking for?"

"Well now Vince, we'll know that when we find it, won't we?" With that he made arrangements to see the Chief of Detectives about the leak from their department. As he turned out his desk lamp to go home there was something about the description he'd heard that made his hair tingle. It was the eyes, the description of the eyes, that he'd have to remember.

17.

A few nights later Don dropped into the little supper club where he had met Irene. He couldn't stay away from the street too long because his information source would dry up. After he had ordered a drink he engaged the bartender in some casual conversation. What he heard caused him to freeze; his chest and stomach literally turning to ice. For a few seconds he couldn't believe his ears. The bartender continued to rattle on, oblivious to the effect his words had on Don.

"Yeah, the word's out all over on the basic description of the sniper. I understand the Organization must want him more than the police. I certainly wouldn't want to have them after me." The bartender completed his story.

Don, now in complete control of his emotions again, asked casually, "Just how did they describe this guy they're looking for anyway?"

The bartender said, "Actually from what I heard, he could be a thousand different guys in this city. Average weight and height, blue eyes and brown hair, not too young. They feel he's a loner."

Don could feel the freezing constriction in his chest again. They were close, very close. He had to get away from here and to a place where he could think things through. So far everything had gone smoothly. He'd known going to the warehouse was a risk but it was the only way. Now he needed more information and to get it he would have to take more risks. He paid for his drink and left the bar, his mind more than a little cluttered with his thoughts and a tightness in his stomach that came from the knowledge that he was being pursued.

He walked into Benotti's supper club; it was about 7:30 P.M. and the dining room was mostly empty. At the bar there were a couple of other customers; looked like a slow night. He took a seat and ordered a drink. The bartender did a double take but brought the drink. As he placed it in front of Don he nervously asked, "How's the wife? I haven't seen you in a few weeks." Something in his manner shot warning signals through Jason's head. He answered as casually as he could, "She's all right. I'm just having a quicky on my way home; the kids worry her too."

He saw what appeared to be relief cross the bartender's face, like a load had been lifted from his back. "So you have children. I'll bet you enjoy them; I do mine," answered the bartender. "Look, I have to leave for a couple of minutes for the john. Will you be okay?"

"Certainly," Don told him as he put down a couple of dollars to cover the drink. But he continued to watch the bartender as he walked away towards the rear of the club. He sensed danger—nothing he could put his finger on—but that feeling the hunted get when they know the enemy is near. After several long minutes, when the bartender still hadn't returned and the other customers were getting restless, the feeling of foreboding became overpowering. The alarm bells were ringing in his ears now and he suddenly felt constricted by the confines of the club. He had to get out. He got up quickly and walked rapidly up the street towards where he had parked his car about a block away. He got about halfway to his car and stopped. He crossed the street and stood in a darkened doorway. He didn't know exactly why but he had to be sure of something.

Within five minutes two cars pulled into the club parking lot. Two men left one of the cars and went into the club. Of the other two, one stayed in the car and the other walked towards the rear of the club. For some reason Don felt at ease now. He was the Hunter again, in control of the situation, at this time anyway. It was obvious to him that his instincts had been correct; the bartender had called someone. How had he made a connection? From the description or just a lucky guess? Whatever, he realized now they had an excellent description and knew his alias. They were close indeed.

The four men returned to their cars and drove away. Don

watched them as the cars disappeared down the street. He remained in the doorway another fifteen minutes. When nothing more happened he walked to where his car was parked and drove away. As he was heading home, he thought, "I have to get away from here. They may make another connection and I'll be a goner." He sat up suddenly, grasping the steering wheel tightly, completely alert. Christ, he had forgotten about Irene for the moment! She was another connection for the bartender had referred to his wife. She was now in mortal danger herself from her contact with him. Was this the way the rest of his life would be, bringing misery and sorrow to anyone he became involved with? Now fear really gripped him; not for himself but for Irene who could be injured or killed and never know what happened to her or why.

He had a real problem. How could he help her without endangering himself? She really knew nothing about him. She didn't even know where he lived or where he supposedly worked. He owed her nothing. As a lover she had been delightful, but did he really owe her? She had received as much as she gave, two lonely people having found some moments of happiness in their troubled worlds. Maybe if he stayed away from her they might never discover her identity. He threw this thought away immediately. If the bartender had given his description to those people, then he had as surely given them hers too. He felt extremely ill. It was a responsibility he didn't want. It was dangerous enough to protect himself, but how could he protect her? How much could he tell her, or could he tell her anything? If she stayed in the city she would certainly get caught. Why hadn't he considered this possibility before? No time for remorse. What was done was done. He had to come up with something, some way, to help her.

* * *

Angelo Conti was a passenger in one of the two cars that had driven away from the club. He spoke to the driver of the car. "Did you get that feeling back there like we were

101

being watched?" The driver only grunted a negative. "I sure did," continued Angelo. "The weirdest feeling I've had in weeks. My instinct tells me we're after the right guy. I was there when Joe got it and I have the same feeling now. If that creepy bartender hadn't fouled up the whole deal we'd have caught him. I know it." Still the driver said nothing. Conti continued, "We've got to report to the boss right away. This guy is still tracking us. Who could be next? Not me I hope. I'm small potatoes."

The driver finally spoke up. "Shut your trap you shit head. You talk too much. I don't feel nothing and I'm not worried about nothing. We go see Aaron and tell him and let him do the worrying. Now leave me in peace."

Conti felt the sting of the rebuff. So he had blabbed a little to the police after Joe's death. They weren't there; they didn't know what it was like to be talking with a guy and suddenly his brains are all over the car. He hadn't told the cops anything they didn't already know. Mr. Greenblatt had told him to forget it. But he just couldn't shake that weird feeling he'd had in the supper club. He had to smile his wicked little smile when he thought of the terrified bartender. If he had snapped his fingers, I'm sure he'd have shit his pants. Mr. Greenblatt was right, keep the little shits scared and they stayed in line.

They pulled up to Benotti's old restaurant and parked on the street. Aaron Greenblatt would be there waiting for their report. It was with no little trepidation they walked inside to announce their failure. Marco Benotti didn't like that kind of news. Aaron was sitting at a table near the rear with Damoni and another man was sitting with him. They were having a cup of coffee and obviously had been waiting for the two enforcers. Without preamble, Greenblatt asked—more a statement than a question—"So where you got him stashed? That was quick work." His cold black eyes bored through Conti like a laser beam through steel.

Conti cleared his throat; he felt so intimidated by this man, he could hardly speak as he croaked out, "We didn't get him. He split before we got there."

None of the three at the table spoke. Each had his eyes on Conti and he felt so inadequate. Why did they have to stare like that? Greenblatt finally broke the silence. "So we sent a couple of boys to do a man's work. What's this outfit coming to when you can't get dependable people?"

Conti finally found his voice. "That's not quite right Mr. Greenblatt. It was the bartender. He made the guy suspicious and he split a couple of minutes before we got there. The damn bartender was so scared he'd give anything away. He was actually green around the eyes. We didn't come away completely empty-handed though." He then paused, waiting to see what happened next.

He didn't wait long. Greenblatt almost shouted at him. "So now I'm a dentist or something and have to pull every bit of information from you like pulling teeth? You got something to say, say it."

Conti lost what composure he had gained and nervously told them about the woman. "She's about 5 feet 6 inches, 125, brown hair and about 35 to 40 years old. The bartender is almost certain they are married and have kids. There's a chance he's not the one we want after all."

Greenblatt responded, "So we got a description of her, maybe we can get to him through her. There's something about this whole deal that bothers me. I'm going to have to report to Marco about this. If you got there as soon as you say you did why didn't you check the neighborhood? Maybe he didn't have a chance to get away."

Conti and the driver looked at each other and Conti finally answered. "We didn't think of that. As soon as we found he was not in the club we came back to report immediately. If it means anything, I did have the distinct impression someone was watching us. He'll never come back there again if he was the guy."

Greenblatt just looked for a few seconds. "Oy Veh! They didn't think of checking the neighborhood. He has the feeling they were being watched. When this guy walks up and hands you a basket to hold while he puts your head in it you'll probably help him." He had a very pained expression on his face. "Now I gotta tell Benotti we probably had him and a couple of schleps let him get away. Yes, I agree with you. If he was our man he'll never be back." He dismissed the two and with a deep sigh headed for the telephone in the rear. Conti and the driver walked out with a sigh of relief. Their ordeal was over, at least for the moment.

*   *   *

Bob Fletcher of *The News* was lounging in Donelly's office long after normal working hours. He was slouched in a chair in the corner, nursing a cup of coffee, watching a harried Donelly leafing through a case file. "Christ, Lieutenant, you put in more hours than a city editor. Don't you ever take a break?"

Fletcher was one of those tall, raw-boned types you associated with the old west. He looked completely out of place as a reporter. Maybe it was his open, innocent face that elicited trust from the great as well as the small. He had been a newspaperman for years and was highly respected in his craft. Donelly looked at him and thought, "Who would believe this is one of the best? He looks like he hasn't bought a new suit since 1950 and that hat, Christ, it must be as old as he is." He couldn't remember when he hadn't worn it. He also knew that behind that facade of country bumpkin was a mind as sharp as any he had ever encountered. The one thing Donelly respected in anyone, man or woman, was a good mind, no matter what else they may appear to be. Maybe that's why he and Fletcher had gotten along so well over the years. It was why he thought Fletcher deserved an answer now.

Fletcher was mildly surprised when he got one. "If I take a break I'll fall so far behind I'll never catch up. Sometimes I think all we have here is a criminal element." He reached out and sipped some cold coffee, made a distasteful expression and shoved the cup away.

"Have you made any headway on the sniper? He's real news. You think he's finished or will he strike again? You know I'm not going to let it drop. I smell a story here that's sensational."

104

Donelly looked over at Fletcher and leaned back in his chair, stretching his arms over his head and then clasping his hands behind his neck. He and Fletcher had been through a lot together and had a certain amount of professional regard for one another. The hard lines of stress around his eyes and mouth softened slightly as he contemplated his answer. "Look at this desk and you ask me about one case. Come on Fletch, I'm busier than a one-eyed, three-legged mouse in a room full of cats."

Fletcher continued to watch him for some sign he'd recognize. "We've known each other a long time," he said. "Why don't you unofficially bounce something off me just to see what happens.?"

Donelly thought for a few seconds before answering. "Strictly off the record and I don't want it repeated. There's a leak in here somewhere. I think I know where it is but I need proof. It seems the Organization finds out any new information as soon as I do. There have been a couple of times they even knew something before I did. That's why I haven't discussed anything about that case. Actually it's more or less on a back burner for now though Vince and I work on it a little each day. I can't say we're making progress because I don't really know what it is I'm looking for or if I'll recognize it when I do."

Fletcher prompted him a little. "Do you feel the sniper is a Galahad or a Son of Sam? Public opinion was pretty much behind him in our last survey."

"You know, Fletch," Donelly answered, "I lean towards the Galahad. There are a number of influential people who disagree and are giving me migraines, but I hold my original theory. I feel there is one mad customer out there who's not through, but when he is we'll know it. He's taking revenge for some real or imagined hurt and when he's extracted his vengeance he'll stop. There, I've said it. You're the only one I've ever told that to so keep it under your hat. The people here will think I'm whacko."

Fletcher thought over what Donelly had said. "If your

theory is correct the sniper could be anyone—not an Organization-related thing at all."

"That's what bothers me," answered Donelly. "Everything points to a professional hit but my instincts, or whatever you want to call them, tell me it's not. If I were a woman you could call it intuition."

Fletcher came back. "So far those killed have been troops in the trenches. Wouldn't this indicate prior knowledge of who he was after. I understand the Organization's goons are walking around looking over their shoulders. In a way, whoever it is, is doing us—and you—a big favor. I happen to be for capital punishment, Mom's apple pie, law and order and anything else you can mention. But I'm still on his side."

Donelly heaved himself up and went to warm up his coffee. The dialogue with Fletcher hadn't gotten out of hand yet and he wanted a couple of minutes to clear his thoughts before they continued. When he returned Fletcher hadn't moved. The guy was starting to become a fixture. After Donelly sat down he said, "I believe in capital punishment myself. It's a two-way street. This sniper, whoever he is, has to be stopped and made to pay his bill too." With this, Fletcher finally sat upright in his chair. "If the guy is doing such a good job for you why try to stop him? You know the only ones being hurt are people long deserving."

Donelly answered, "What kind of policeman would I be if I didn't try to stop this guy? To a policeman it can't matter who is being murdered. Murder is murder. I don't feel I'm the one to be judge and jury in this case. I just find them. It's someone else's job to judge."

"Most of our readers feel the guy has been doing a public service, not so far removed from the old style vigilantes."

Donelly thought that one over. "I know what the public opinion polls say but I say again that the man—or men—have to be found. I want to get them before the Organization does simply for their own protection. I'm almost certain it's only one guy, and he's good. So far he hasn't left a trace of his existence at any crime site. All we have to go on now is word of mouth descriptions from a witness who really didn't get that good a look at him. If I catch him he'll at least get a fair trial. If they catch him, I'm afraid he'll get a terminal illness."

"I'm not trying to sway your opinion," Fletcher replied. "I happen to agree with you actually." He yawned. "It's an extraordinary case, but it's late. Enough philosophizing for one night. It hurts my head. I'll let you get some work done so you can go home too." He shrugged himself out of his chair, walked out of the office and down the hallway.

Donelly watched the retreating figure of the newsman. "What would I do if I knew who the sniper was?" he wondered. "It's an interesting question. I hate the fuckers with a passion and so far he's taken care of three particularly vicious ones." He shifted his mental gears slightly and began re-reading the description they had obtained through his informant. There was something vaguely familiar about the description but it fit so many people. The case files he had been going through hadn't helped much. Monero had unearthed a wealth of information, almost too much. It could be confusing and a lot of it misleading. He returned to his original thoughts. What would he do if he ran this fellow to ground? In a way he wished they would never find him, but the cop in him said he must. He had to get home and get some rest. Maybe tomorrow he could get a fresh perspective on the thing. If only he didn't have so many other open cases cluttering up his mind. They sometimes started running together. He left his office and ambled down the semi-dark hallway where only the night shift still had their lights on.

18.

With the realization the Organization had such an accurate description of him, Roberts knew he would have to move. It was just too dangerous to remain in the area where he had been living since there were so many underworld-type characters there and it was only a matter of time until one of them would make a connection and set the dogs on him. The bartender at Benotti's club could make a positive identification if he chanced to meet him on the street, or in a store, or anywhere. He felt confident he could take care of himself by just staying on the move, but what would he do about Irene? He had decided he couldn't just leave her unaware of the possible danger. If, by chance, she met the bartender. . . . He couldn't bear the consequences.

He packed the few items he had brought with him when he moved into the apartment. It had been a furnished flat so all he had was some clothing and a few small personal items. He drove out of town for perhaps 20 or 25 miles and checked into a motel, then returned to the apartment and loaded up all his camping gear. He was ready. He went downstairs, stood before the superintendent's door, and knocked. The door opened and the super eyed him suspiciously, as he had been doing the last few times he had seen him. Roberts told him he'd have to move because his Company wanted him back in St. Louis for a three month training program. He told him that if it were possible he'd like an apartment again when he returned. The super said fine, if there was a vacancy he'd be glad to let him have it; he had been a good tenant.

Roberts had one last thing to take care of before leaving. He went back to his apartment and, starting in the kitchenette, washed or wiped everything he could conceivably have touched during his stay. He methodically went from room to room. It took all the rest of that day and much of the night. He finished near the front door, just as he had planned. The flat was spotless; he hadn't even left an old newspaper. He departed just as he had come, alone and silently.

*　　　　*　　　　*

The apartment superintendent had watched his departure. In a way he hated to see him go for he had been a good tenant—one of the only ones who paid his rent promptly and on time. He started thinking back. How long had he been here? He went up to the empty apartment to check it out before renting it again. Walking in, he was amazed. He had never seen one of his rentals so clean. After he thoroughly looked about it out and could find nothing wrong or missing he locked the front door and went to his own apartment. As he sat at his kitchen table drinking a beer he did some thinking. There were a lot of items that added up. The guy was a relative newcomer to town, he was a loner, and he pretty much filled the description he had heard at the local bar a few nights earlier. Why hadn't he made the connection before now? The immaculate apartment had been the key which unlocked his knowledge. He picked up the phone. You never know, maybe someday he'd need a favor.

*　　　　*　　　　*

Roberts drove back to the little motel and slept through the night. He was bone weary from the work and worry of the day before. He looked out the window. It was going to be a beautiful day. The sun was already high in the sky. He looked at his watch, almost 9 A.M. He had to get a move on as he still had a lot to do. On the drive up here yesterday he had done a lot of thinking. It was time for Don Roberts to return to the grave. He had served his purpose well but now it was time to end this masquerade for the hounds on his trail were starting to bay. He could hear them in the distance.

He drove back to the city and closed out his safety deposit box. When he emptied the contents of the box he realized he hadn't spent that much. Of the $50,000 he had

109

started out with there was a good $40,000 left. Once he walked from the bank all his connections with the city would be severed, except for Irene. He still hadn't decided what to do as far as she was concerned. He drove out of the city and headed for his bank in Benson. It had been months since he was here. He was now dressed in his suit and tie for Jason Knorr was returning. At least for awhile. He went by the post office. There were only two letters for him. One from the hospital and one from his insurance company. The letter from the insurance company he placed in his safety deposit box. The letter from the hospital only told him there had been no change in his wife's condition and in the opinion of the doctors there was no hope for recovery. He crumpled up the letter and threw it into the trash.

*   *   *

As Jason Knorr, he purchased a late model car and transferred all his belongings to it. He took the car he had bought as Roberts and drove into the mountains after changing into work clothes and walking boots. He knew exactly where he was going, having checked the area carefully months before. When he reached the place he was seeking he thoroughly scouted it out again. He went over the car just as he had the apartment, carefully wiping everything. He took his binoculars and looked over the area again. No one. He started the engine, put a rock under the accelerator, then placed the car in gear. It lurched forward and over the edge of a sharp precipice, plunging about 75 feet through the air and landing in a bottomless lake. Jason watched it slowly disappear beneath the surface. With his binoculars he surveyed the surroundings again. No one had seen anything. With a tree branch he swept the surface where the car had went over, not leaving a trace. He took Roberts' license and the title for the car and burned them. Roberts had returned to the limbo from whence he came. He started the long hike back to the highway, just a happy hiking bird watcher.

As he walked along the paths and country roads he observed the scenery. He felt in high spirits, realizing he would again be camping out. The forests and hilly country were beautiful. Strange, he thought, that we are in such a hurry in this life, that we sometimes lose contact with nature and its loveliness. He resolved that if he managed to live through the next few weeks he would not miss the wilderness again. From this time on he would spend at least a portion of each year somewhere in the mountains. He looked up and the sky was blue and clear; only a wisp of clouds here and there. The air was clean and pure and as he walked along he inhaled deeply. It was great to be alive. He descended from the foothills and at last came to the highway.

Crossing the highway he continued downhill following an old footpath. He knew the road made several sharp curves as it led down into the valley below but he would save time and distance by walking in a more or less straight line. He had a second reason for doing this: he didn't want to meet anyone on the road who might remember him. While he felt his hike to be quite innocent, he still preferred to avoid contact if it was possible.

By the time he had reached the valley and recrossed the highway again it was getting dark. He would arrive back at his motel in time for supper. The thought made hunger pangs seize him and he quickened his pace. He wanted to be back before nightfall since he didn't want to attract attention by wandering around in the dark. On the way to the motel he passed a diner and, on impulse, turned in and ate his supper there. After eating he realized how tired he was and how late it was getting. He hurried on down the highway to the motel and much needed rest.

19.

When the call had come in from the apartment manager, Aaron Greenblatt dispatched Conti at once to check it out. The super was beside himself with self-importance. He hoped the right people would remember he had cooperated, etcetera, etcetera. This type of groveling made Conti sick but you had to put up with it. Sure, he'd make sure the right people heard about it, just tell me what you know. After listening to the manager Conti was certain it was their man. Now he had the guy's name and he knew he drove an older model red Chevrolet. From this point on it would be duck soup to pick him up. The story of a traveling salesman was obviously a ploy to throw them off the trail. He had to get back and report to Greenblatt. They had to get after this guy immediately.

When he and his companion returned to the restaurant, Conti was dumbstruck for a moment or two. Christ, the big boss, Benotti himself, was there. Conti was so nervous he could hardly stammer out his report. After he finished Benotti told him, "You did good. I appreciate good people. Now how do we go about finding this Donald Roberts?"

Getting increasingly bold because of the compliment Conti suggested, "We can put out the word all over town. Someone will surely know him. We can also check all the hotels and motels. He has to stay somewhere."

Looking a little pained, Benotti realized he had to answer like a schoolmaster instructing young pupils. "No, but we'll do it the easy way. This time we'll let our friends downtown do the looking. They have excellent facilities for that sort of thing. What you want to do is leak the information to them and let them carry the ball."

Conti looked very impressed. What a sharp guy. It made you realize how he got to where he's at. It was very clever. He smiled a conspiratorial smile and said he'd take care of that little item at once. Then he and his buddy scuttled out to do what they had been told.

Benotti turned to Aaron. "He's young but he looks like a good boy. Keep an eye on him. We're going to need replacements in our enforcement group."

*   *   *

It was about an hour later that Monero came into Lieutenant Donelly's office. "You got a call on line three. The guy won't talk to anyone but you. Says he owes you."

Donelly picked up the phone, identified himself, listened for about a minute, and then hung up. Vince stood waiting as Donelly stared into space for a few moments. His ears were getting red and Monero knew he was going into a slow burn. At last he spoke. "Well, we now know who we're looking for. All we have to do is find him. The sniper's name is Donald Roberts and he drives a 1972 red Chevrolet Impala. I want you to get with Department of Motor Vehicles and get an address for this guy. I also want you to get an accurate description from his driver's license application."

Monero nodded that he understood. He said, "Strange they would give us so much information. You'd think they want him bad enough to look themselves."

Donelly replied, "It stinks. Why should they expend the energy when as soon as we know where to find him they'll know too? Let us do the leg work. I also have an address where he's been living for the past few months. I want the lab people to meet us there after you put Motor Vehicles into motion." With that Monero went out to call about the car and license while Donelly made arrangements with the lab to meet them at the empty apartment.

*   *   *

A short time later they were standing in the apartment with the super flitting nervously about. He couldn't really add any information they didn't already have. Roberts had kept pretty much to himself. He was a jogger. The manager remembered that almost every day he had gone to the park to run. He was a salesman and this had explained his long absences from town. He didn't really know where he worked except he sold grinding tools and abrasives to industrial

113

companies. He had said he was returning to St. Louis to attend a training program. Donelly could sense Roberts' presence even though he had departed. This was their man, he was certain. The lab people would be there for hours but the preliminary report was that the place was so clean you could eat off the floor. Donelly told them to do their best for they were grasping at straws. Anything would help.

When they returned to Headquarters Donelly had a message to call Motor Vehicles. He phoned and the sergeant told him that yes, indeed, a Donald Roberts owned a 1972 Chevrolet license number HCG 137. His address didn't surprise Donelly since that was just where he'd been minutes before. He felt his incipient ulcer growl. The driver's license gave him accurate information. Roberts was 5 feet, 11 inches, 170, brown hair and blue eyes; his license number was such and such and his Social Security number was 075-32-9931. He had been born in Carmel, Missouri on January 14, 1932. Donelly told Monero that he was sure they were working with a ghost. "I want an All Points Bulletin on the car and on Roberts. Maybe we'll get lucky. I also want you to run this Social Security number through the Feds to see what we turn up." Monero left to start his assigned tasks.

*   *   *

When he returned to Benson late that night Jason Knorr went to his motel room and fell, exhausted, into a deep sleep. The past three days had been physically demanding and the emotional pressure on him had been immense. He needed the rest. It might be the last chance he'd have for a good night's sleep in a long time so he wanted to make the best of it.

The next morning he was awake early. He felt great, put on his jogging suit and went for a run. He liked running because he was alone and it gave him plenty of time to think. The fresh morning air cleared his lungs and made his whole being feel vital and ready for anything. After he completed his run he returned to the motel, showered and shaved. He went to the restaurant for breakfast. All the thinking he had done about Irene had not resolved anything. He would like her to be safe but to really make sure she was, he'd have to expose himself.

He didn't feel he could place his secret and his life in anyone else's hands. If he explained to her why he wanted her to do certain things to protect herself she would want to know why and he wasn't prepared to tell her. It was a difficult decision but it had to be made; she would have to shift for herself. He had told her at their last meeting he would have to go to St. Louis for training and after that he would have a job where he didn't have to travel any longer. It seemed to satisfy her, but it made no difference anyway. They had no hold on each other. He had told her he would call her every week and hoped this would keep her out of circulation until he was finished with his task. He knew he had made the right decision even if it appeared callous. His single-minded purpose was to extract his revenge. Nothing or no one would be allowed to jeopardize his chance of success. As long as Irene stayed away from the supper club she would be all right. The chance of her making an accidental contact with someone who might recognize her would not justify the risk involved if he let her know his secret. It was enough he would have to live with the knowledge of what he had done. She, however, deserved better than that. If he got away with it, he could always send for her. If he didn't, it wouldn't matter anyway.

After he finished breakfast he drove back into the hills again. He had to have a place to stay and this would be as good as any. He could drive to the city within an hour and no one would pay any attention to a camper in the woods. He wouldn't be doing any more firing so noise or watchers would be no problem. The one thing that bothered him was that he'd have to carry the weapon and ammunition at all times for he couldn't risk someone stealing that while he was away. Everything else was expendable. He would have to be extremely careful not to be stopped for a traffic violation. After he prepared his camp site he constructed a place in the spare tire well which would hold the rifle. This way the case would not be exposed to tempt a casual thief when he had to leave the car parked and unprotected. The next morning he would begin his final hunt.

*   *   *

The next day he was up early and loaded all unnecessary items in the car. On the way to the city he'd stop by the warehouse and add these items to those already stored there. He cleaned up his area, hung his foodstuffs to keep the animals away from them, closed the tent and was ready to travel. He stopped at Benson and unloaded the car at the warehouse. As he rummaged through the crates, memories came flooding back. He had to harden himself and complete the task quickly. No remorse, no regrets, he must continue his quest until he was finished.

After he left the warehouse he drove to the city. This time he wanted to check out Benotti's old restaurant. He realized he couldn't go inside but he could observe as much as he wanted from outside. He had also started a mustache, which altered his appearance a little; not much for someone who knew him well but it should do for anyone else. It was only a couple of weeks old but was already starting to look pretty full. He drove to a spot about a block away and parked the car. He wanted to walk around a bit and try and get the feel of the area.

It was in the old part of town. The street were narrow and tenements crowded to the edge of the sidewalk on each side of the street; a typical ethnic neighborhood in a large city. The restaurant itself was crammed between two apartment houses. If a customer drove his car here he would be extremely lucky to find a place to park. It was a neighborhood restaurant and bar. No wonder Benotti felt safe when he was here. As he walked he could feel eyes upon him. He was recognized immediately as a stranger. He realized this would never do for what he had planned. To help allay suspicions he stopped at a little deli and bought a salami. He then purposefully returned to his car and drove away, hop-

116

ing it would appear to anyone watching him that he was just another outsider that had come down to get some real Italian delicatessen. As he drove off he could feel the sweat running down his back. It was the cold sweat of fear. He knew he had made a mistake, one he'd be more careful of in the future. He should have realized beforehand the type of neighborhood Benotti would have been from. It was beginning to appear that it might be impossible to get close enough to Benotti to complete his quest.

*　　　*　　　*

That evening, through the neighborhood grapevine, Marco Benotti heard about the alien that had been in the neighborhood. From the brief description he was given he and his lieutenants decided to discount his presence. It wasn't that strange that people came into this area and made purchases at the deli. It did make him feel good that the old neighborhood system was still working. It had served him well as a youth and would as he grew older. The cops could never figure out how, as youths, he and his friends always knew when they were near. It gave a guy a real comfortable feeling. There was, of course, something else that did not make him feel comfortable. As a matter of fact, it pained him to think they couldn't resolve the problem of the mysterious sniper. This had been the purpose of his visit to the restaurant in the first place.

Aaron was reporting to him on progress or, more accurately, the lack of progress at this very moment. All their channels seemed to be stymied on this one. They had to make a breakthrough somehow. This character couldn't be allowed to get away.

"The police don't know from shit," Aaron said. "I have their reports on the investigation of this Roberts and it's nothing. The only place he seems to have existed is at the apartment house. The name is an obvious alias. The trail starts and stops right at that address. They are checking with the FBI and the Social Security Administration but I'll bet they come up with zilch."

117

Benotti thought this over. "Aaron, we can't let this guy get away with what he's done. It's been weeks now since he made a hit. Maybe he's through, but we're not. I want this guy found if it takes forever. Has anyone heard anything about the woman? I have a feeling she was just a pickup and probably wouldn't know anything anyway."

"I tend to agree with you," replied Aaron, "This guy is good. I don't feel he'd confide in anyone. He's strictly a loner. If we could just figure out why he was doing it we'd be a long way towards solving who he is. The police so far haven't been any help and my contact is really getting nervous. He feels Donelly is keeping information in his head and not putting it in reports any more. He doesn't want to pressure too much, get too curious, or he may be uncovered. That wouldn't be any good for any of us."

"It's those Queens of Spades. I've asked all around but nobody seems to know anything," Benotti continued. "I even went to old Gina, the witch lady. You remember her from when we were kids?"

"Yeah, everyone was afraid of her. Christ she must be older than dirt. What did she tell you?" asked Aaron.

"In the old days people wanting to extract revenge always sent a marker of some sort so the victim would know why he was getting it and she feels this is the significance of the cards. She did say because it was the Queen she feels there is a woman involved. The Spade suit, of course, means death. She said it was a husband, son, or father extracting revenge for a woman in his life. She said we should look to this possibility in our search. The last thing she said is what really bothers me. There will be more death; she sees it in my future. She didn't know who or wouldn't say. That's why I say we have to get this guy."

Their dinner had arrived so they started eating. Most conversation ended except for a little small talk. The wine was excellent and, of course, the service was the best. After the meal, over cigars and coffee, Damoni said, "We've got another problem cropping up. We've started to get a little lip over at collections. People are losing confidence in us."

118

"Well we'll just have to start leaning harder," Benotti replied. "We can't let our system break down because of one clown out there taking potshots. Now is when we really got to stick together. I want you all to tighten up your act right now and nip this problem in the bud." Everyone agreed that this was the thing to do and would start immediately. The meal ended on a fairly happy note with Benotti feeling he at least had his people back on the right track. The things old Gina had told him were almost forgotten in the euphoria of comradeship.

20.

It was a week later when Lieutenant Donelly received an answer from Social Security. The name Roberts and the number didn't match. There was a good chance the number had come from a box top. It meant nothing. The FBI was also disappointing. Unless they could come up with fingerprints there wasn't much they could do. The name Donald Roberts was a fairly common name. Donelly hadn't really expected anything else. The way this case had been going why expect any kind of break? It was time to go back to the drawing board and start on a new track. The related cases he and Vince had been working on weren't providing much satisfaction either. They had just about beat every scrap of information they had to death and still nothing. He felt the answer lay in these of cases but he just couldn't find the connection. He decided to try one more long shot.

He placed a long distance call to the Bureau of Records in Carmel, Missouri. It was a desperation move and unorthodox but right now he'd try anything. When the clerk answered he asked her if she could research her birth records for January 14, 1932 and see if a Donald Roberts was recorded that day. She told him to hang on; it would take a while to go through the ledgers. After what seemed hours she came back on the line. "Lieutenant Donelly, we do have a birth recorded for that name on that date."

Donelly wasn't sure he heard right. Could he be so lucky? "Do you have a death recorded for him or do you have any idea how I could contact him?"

"I'm afraid not, Lieutenant, other than the birth there is no record of him," she answered. "You could try the police, they might know something."

Donelly thanked her and placed a call to the local police department. After a few minutes of social amenities they got around to business. "There was a man named Donald Roberts born in Carmel on January 14, 1932," Donelly said. "I have checked with the Bureau of Records but that's all they know about him. Do you have any information on him?"

It was a few minutes before the Chief replied. "Funny you'd ask about him. He was a citizen here until he went into the Army around the time of Korea. While he was gone his mother died and it was my understanding he was killed in action over there. He was the last of the family. Sort of tragic, in a way. Why do you ask?"

"His name, or what appears to be his name, showed up in a case I'm working on. I wanted to cover all bases which is why I called. You've been a tremendous help to me. If you ever get over this way drop in and I'll buy you dinner."

After he hung up Donelly sat and thought over what he had learned. He now had one piece of information no one else in the city had. Roberts had actually existed; he was not a figment of someone's imagination. He had died an orphan so it was likely there was a connection some time while he was in the service, before he was killed. This was one he would sit on. He wouldn't even tell Monero. He had a premonition he was on the verge of discovering the sniper's real identity. If he did, what would he do with the information? But first he had to make the connection. He would have Vince go through all the old files and cover service records like a blanket. Only he would know what he was actually looking for and he was not about to tell anyone.

*   *   *

It was raining and miserable laying in this small patch of woods, but the Hunter didn't mind. He had been observing traffic along a short stretch of road in the suburbs. This was the second day in a row he had been here. He arrived early, before dawn, and remained concealed until darkness set in. He had constructed a simple blind from which he could observe and felt a person would have to step on him to know he was there. He was soaked to the bone, and cold, but he had to be sure he could get the job done from here. It was just a little more than a hundred yards from his position to the quiet boulevard to his front. He picked this loca-

121

tion because of a gentle curve that made the cars stay in his view for an extra second or two.

Another reason he was here was that this was one of three routes utilized by Benotti's driver to go into the city. He had rechecked everything. Benotti seldom came to the new restaurant where he had gotten Gallagher. He didn't leave his car until he was in an underground garage at his office. And the old restaurant was impossible. He'd never get in and out undetected. It was either this or try at home. If he did the job here it would be a moving target, but that was no big thing. He'd done it before and the range here would be minimal. At a hundred yards he should pick the eye out of a gnat, he smiled, or the head off a cockroach. He was sure he could do it but he'd just have to wait until he came this way. That would be the hard part: the wait. As Benotti only had three routes common sense told him that at least once a week he'd come this way. On the fourth day of his vigil he was rewarded. It was a Wednesday morning a little after 9 A.M.

As he watched the car approach, he recognized it immediately. It was scrupulously obeying the speed laws and was traveling approximately 25 miles an hour. The limousine cruised around the curve and the Hunter watched through his binoculars. Perfect. He could see Benotti plain as day though the windows of the car. He was in the rear seat and had one guy beside him, one in the front seat, plus the driver. No matter, by the time they could react he'd be two or three hundred yards away in his car.

He felt he was now ready for the final act. He would mail the last card. He hated to think Benotti would die and not know why. But how to tell him? He couldn't send him a note because that could be traced by a handwriting expert. Did the scum really need to know? He would be answering for unknown hundreds of people. It gave the Hunter a feeling of elation that his quest was nearing its end and he would be avenging many wrongs. When this was over he'd again lay down the sword as he had done once before. It would be a job well done. While not particularly liking what he was doing, someone had to do it, and he felt he had been selected. He returned to his campsite and prepared the letter. The next day he drove into the city and mailed it. He then drove through his old neighborhood and back to his campsite. The next night he would call Irene.

He had made it a point to call her at least once a week. He wanted to allay her fears and maybe keep her off the streets and at home. Once he got to Benotti he felt she would no longer be a threat to him and maybe he could tell her a part of the story. If they lived and lived together . . . yes! That's what he wanted to do . . . he'd have to tell her something. His big problem would be, could he walk away after Benotti?

*   *   *

On Monday morning it was panicsville at the Organization's headquarters. Benotti looked at the Queen of Spades and turned green. This was the ultimate insult. Who would dare attack him? This guy had to be out of his tree. He sent for his lieutenants immediately. Things were getting out of hand. He had no idea of what they could do that they weren't already doing. Why hadn't the stinking police found this nut? He'd provided them with a name, a description and an address. He was extremely confused. Everytime he looked at the card he felt the fear grip his chest. He had to get a hold of his nerves before the others arrived; it wouldn't do to let them know he was scared. His guts felt like jelly and his mouth was dry but outwardly he appeared composed.

They showed up one at a time and after they were all assembled Benotti passed the card around to each of them. It was identical to the one Peroni had received. No one wanted to hold it. It was like something vile and evil, something you didn't want to associate with if it was possible to avoid it. After they had all examined the card they sat and waited for instructions.

This time Benotti had lost a little bluster. "We all know

what this means. Apparently I'm to be the next victim of this nut. I do not intend to become a victim. I want this guy found and quick. I'm going to have to stay out of sight a few days of course. We'll conduct our business by phone. We know this guy is good but he can't possibly be better than our entire organization." He looked around the table. Was it possible one of these people were responsible? You couldn't tell from their expressions; each had that complete blank that was almost their code.

Damoni was the first to answer. "Boss, we've pulled out every stop we know. This guy's an unknown quantity. I'm certain he's an amateur in this business and his luck is bound to run out. He's a complete mystery to any of our street people. I don't know what else to tell you except we'll keep trying."

The others nodded assent at this statement but today Benotti was not to be so easily mollified. This time it was his head on the block. He had the power, and he was going to use it. "Bullshit," he shouted, "I'm getting tired of listening to these Goddamn fairy tales. I want some action. Spend whatever you need, strong arm anyone around, but get on top of this guy. He can't just disappear and reappear anytime he damn well pleases. Aaron, I don't care if that cop buddy of yours gets hung by the testicles, I want to know what the police know about this case."

Aaron looked very downcast. "Marco, we've been friends for years and I've never let you down, but exposing this guy could close our pipeline for years. We promised him we'd protect him. This will mean the end of him. Are you sure we should take such a drastic step?"

Marco was almost beside himself. "As you say, Aaron, we've been friends for years. Are you ready to see me go down the tubes or are you going to expose some cheap stool pigeon. That Donelly is too smug. I know he knows something he's not telling and we've got to know what it is."

Aaron finally knuckled under. "Okay, Marco. I don't think he really knows that much or at least he certainly hasn't acted on it yet. But I'll let my contact know it's time to collect all debts."

The others around the table all nodded assent. The business had been hurt a little as a result of this problem and if dumping one dumb cop to bring it to a head was the price, it was a bargain. Others could always be bought. It wasn't the end of the world. Damoni had been watching Marco closely. He didn't like the look of pallor about his face and eyes. It was obvious he was worried. He spoke up. "Marco, maybe you should take a vacation. Get out and get some sun for a few days. While you're gone, perhaps we'll get the break we need to crack this and get it over with."

At this Benotti really exploded. "Is that it? You want me out of town? You think some cheap hick with a rifle is going to run me out of my town? Maybe that's what you're all thinking, eh? It's a good way to get old Marco out of the way so the mice can play? Not on your life. I'm staying right here. It's business as usual and don't any of you forget it."

Aaron was visibly shaken by the outburst as were the others. "Wait a minute, Marco," he said right away. "No one here wants you out of town but it ain't a bad idea. Remember what you said after Joe got it. This guy obviously follows us around and picks his spot before he mails the card. If you leave town for a couple of days it will change your routine. The other thing I want to mention, you know how dangerous it can be conducting business on the telephone. Think over the suggestion. We don't want to say things under pressure we might be sorry for later."

The calming effect on Benotti was obvious to everyone in the room and they all relaxed a little. "Doggone it, Aaron, you always know the right thing to say. Maybe you're right. I haven't had a vacation in a couple of years. Maybe I'll go to Palm Springs; that's supposed to be real classy." He was smiling again, and at ease. The others were happy with the turn of events. It was all settled; he would leave either the next day or the day after. The time spent away they would

125

play by ear. He would call the state capital and see if their lodge was available. The meeting broke up and Aaron left with a sense of foreboding. He felt he was going to blow a good lead for no useful purpose.

*   *   *

That evening Donelly was sitting in his office. Tonight was his report night for the Chief of Detectives. He knew the sniper would come up and he had nothing new to report. He and Monero had eliminated a number of possibilities but that was about it. He looked at his desk. The remains of a stale chicken sandwich and a carton of milk, his supper, stared back at him. He thought, "The story of my life: cold chicken or hamburger, lines under my eyes and a sickening cough from too many cigarettes. Marco Benotti is having a big steak tonight and I'm doing his dirty work for him." His incipient ulcer growled to let him know he had forgotten something. He and Vince had been going back through the eight cases to get a list of names to check out with the military. He hadn't told Monero why, but he just wanted to see what turned up in the sweep.

It was time to report. He picked up his summaries and headed for the Chief's office. On the way he passed Lieutenant Winters who had just come out. "You got heavy company tonight, pardner. Everyone but the Mayor's there to listen. It's the first time I've seen this since I started reporting." He walked on down the hallway. Donelly's stomach gurgled a couple of more times. He hadn't intended to even mention the sniper but something told him this would be what the whole meeting would be about. He opened the door and went into the room.

The Chief of Detectives was sitting at this desk. He was flanked by Captain Eddy of the Crime Task Force and the Police Commissioner. It was, indeed, heavy company. The room was filled with stale cigar and cigarette smoke. The only lights were a lamp in the corner and the Chief's desk lamp. Donelly had an eerie feeling, like a heretic appearing before the Tribunal. The Chief put him at ease and told him

126

to sit down. He offered him a cup of coffee which Donelly declined. He only wanted to get it over with. He started going down the list. In all the time he had been reporting it was the first time no one had made a comment or asked for clarification on a case. After he completed his report he sat for a few moments and them prepared to leave. The Chief spoke up.

"Just a minute Donelly. You went over this sniper case pretty fast. All I heard was lead eliminations. You don't have anything new?"

Donelly thought to himself, "Here it comes. How can I do this tactfully." He tried to answer evasively. "No sir. We're working on one angle but it's more to eliminate a last possibility than anything else. If it doesn't pan out I'm going to recommend the back burner for it. It's taking too much time."

"You can't do that!" It was blurted out by the Commissioner. Everyone looked at him. He had regained his composure now and said more calmly, "What I meant was, this guy has murdered three citizens and it's news. If the papers find out we've relegated it to a reduced status, they'll have a field day at our expense."

It was a good, quick recovery. Donelly had to admit he was excellent. The political angle really had the element of truth and actual concern in it. They were all aware of their public image. Maybe he was right. What he said to the other three was, "I suppose you're right, Mr. Commissioner, but it is taking up a lot of time and we've exhausted about all our leads. The one I have I would prefer to keep to myself until I'm certain which way it will take me."

Captain Eddy spoke up. "Lieutenant, if you have something definite I have a right to know. I am in charge of the Task Force that's supposed to be keeping an eye on these people. I get the feeling you don't trust someone. Is that right?"

Well he certainly laid it on the table, thought Donelly. I can't possibly lay my hunch out there without getting something in return. He would play his trump card and see who took the bait. "Captain, it isn't that. The lead I'm working on is so nebulous, it's actually a straw in the wind. If I'm right it might lead us somewhere but if it's wrong I don't want to look too foolish. On that basis alone I'd like to be left to work it out alone and see where it takes me. In a couple of days I may have something."

The Chief of Detectives seeing a rift building between the two protagonists spoke up quickly. "Okay, Lieutenant, we'll give you until next week to give us an answer. Then there won't be any dilly-dallying, you understand?"

'Yes, sir. Can I go now?"

"No, wait." It was Eddy again. "I wasn't going to let this out but I suppose I have no choice. Our informants tell us Benotti received a Queen of Spades."

This really dropped like a bomb. For a few seconds the only sound was the wall clock ticking. It had so astounded Donelly that he just couldn't find his tongue. He had a million thoughts and questions but his mind was thoroughly confused for a few seconds. The implication of this information was tremendous. He didn't know why but he was glad he had kept the information about Roberts to himself. If this guy was successful at blowing away Benotti he'd really be doing the community a favor. It also made it imperative he find out who this sniper was though he still wasn't sure what he'd do if he did discover his identity.

The news about Benotti would be certain to make headlines if anyone in the media found out. Donelly was now certain one of the three he had been talking to was the leak from the department. You'd never prove anything against them unless you could force them into the open. He was really banking on the military records to give him a lead to the sniper. The meeting broke up and he returned to his office. He had to find Monero and get him started with this new bit of information. From this point on he knew that it was really going to get interesting.

21.

Days later a news item caught the eye of the hunter. He had been observing Benotti's residence and had noticed the flurry of activity at the main house. Then came the period Benotti or his bodyguards did not appear at the suburban home. He had checked out his business address and still no Benotti. He realized he would take extra precautions after receiving the Queen but to completely disappear? Impossible. Then the paper had run the short story under Bob Fletcher's byline. Benotti was on vacation at a private lodge near Palm Springs. It had, so the story went, been his doctor's order that he get away for reasons of health. The Hunter smiled a tight smile over that for it was certainly the truth. At least he now knew where his prey had gone and why. He just had to bide his time. Benotti wouldn't stay away forever. He took special precautions to only check the downtown office for activity and he avoided his ambush spot entirely.

The interlude gave him an opportunity to return from "St. Louis" for a visit with Irene the following weekend. She was a very astute person and when talking with her he realized his subterfuge wouldn't last forever. If it could only continue this way for a few weeks more, the deception perhaps could end.

In the past few months he had learned a great deal about her. That she was a self-made woman was evident. She had been married while still young but after five years it just hadn't worked out. She and her husband had parted as friends and he still lived back east. After her divorce she had returned to college and received a degree in business administration. She had immediately put it to use, landing a job with a major construction firm and working her way up from minor administrator to her present job as office manager at their main headquarters.

As Don Roberts, Jason realized he was becoming attached to her in a way he had not intended. It was difficult not to be attracted to her. She was extremely good-looking, well-educated, smart, and confident in her abilities and her place in the scheme of things. She was a wonderful companion; easy to get along with, even-tempered, and it made him proud, when they were out, that she drew many admiring glances.

After their long weekend together he left again for "St. Louis," promising himself that someday she would have to know at least part of it.

*   *   *

Benotti and his troops were having a ball. The lodge had been a great idea but he knew eventually he had to return to the city. He couldn't stay away from the business for too long. Other people got too many ideas. No point in providing too much temptation for them. The one thing that bothered him was that for all their contacts his street people couldn't come up with a lead to this sniper character. He was relatively safe; he had enough people around him to stop an army. This guy would find out getting a foot soldier was one thing but getting him would be quite another.

He had talked with Aaron that morning and he had nothing to report. Their contact at Police Headquarters had been unable to force any information. He felt Donelly knew something but wasn't telling anyone. They had given an ultimatum to him and he would have to talk this week so they might find out something that would provide a lead. There had been no sign of the man fitting the description; it was as if he had fallen from the face of the earth. Aaron had a couple of people quietly checking out hotels and motels but they hadn't turned up anything either. He thought it would be safe for Benotti to return. They needed him. A couple of problems had come up in the numbers and some small timers were getting a little too bold in prostitution. Benotti told him he'd be back on Monday and maybe they could knock a few heads.

After he hung up he thought long and hard. Was it possi-

130

ble this was an inside job? His intuition told him it was not, but you had to cover all possibilities. He'd learned mistrust at an early age. You left nothing to chance. Except for his wife he trusted no one and let no one get too close to him. He thought of the old days when he was fighting his way up to the top. He had done his share and a little more. Everyone knew Marco could be counted on and that's why he had prospered. He had money, plenty of it. Maybe he should retire. His kids were all grown now and away from home. It was just he and his wife. It wasn't like the old days anymore. A guy could quit and go away in peace as long as he stayed retired and kept his mouth shut.

He had called Marconi at the capital and had a long talk with him. They had sent in four guys from out of state to help out. Even he didn't know who they were. They were complete unknowns to his people and thus unknown to anyone else too. They were independently looking for this sniper. They were shadowing Benotti from a distance, never making direct contact. For some reason this gave him a great deal of comfort. So far his own people had turned up nothing: always a day late and a dollar short. They would continue to squeeze the police contact. If they found out anything he was to call Marconi and he would get the word to the independents.

One of Marco's cronies broke his train of thought. The girls had shown up and it was party time. He got up from his chair, went outside to the pool and joined the others.

*   *   *

Donelly and Monero sat in Donelly's office. They had been there for hours poring over the information in the old files. They were now five years back into the records; that's as long as the three hoods had worked together. They had come up with a couple of more cases but these had provided no further information. Each person involved in each case had been checked out over and over again. It seemed hopeless. They had split the files in half and after each completed his study they traded. At last Donelly said to Vince,

131

"We're getting nowhere. There doesn't seem to be anyone in these cases interested enought to try revenge, especially against the Organization."

"I know," Vince answered. "The whole thing just doesn't make sense. Do you think it could possibly be some guy who slipped a cog and now feels he's the saviour of the world?"

Donelly hadn't really considered that angle. "It's a possibility, but I'd say a real long shot. There is something that does make me want to check one more item. The method being utilized indicates the guy is a terrific marksman. This suggests a military background to me. I want you to take all these names and run them through the Department of Defense. I also want you to include our three victims and the mysterious non-person Roberts."

Monero looked pained. "That's a lot of ground to cover, boss. How will we trace this Roberts if he doesn't exist?"

Donelly handed him a piece of paper. "Here is his name, birth date, birth place, and a possible social security number. It's what I haven't told anyone else. Keep that in mind. I don't want anyone to know about this."

After looking at the paper Monero broke into a wide grin. "Will do, boss. Maybe we'll come up with something after all."

"I made a call to Carmel, Missouri," Donelly simply replied. "I know now this Roberts did, in fact, exist. He was killed in Korea a long time ago."

Monero was now excited. "So that's why we're going to look for a military connection. It might be the answer. I'll get this letter off right away."

After Monero left, Donelly fingered the stack of files in front of him. "Old friends," he thought, "you're going to give up your answer whether you want to do it or not." Donelly felt rather pleased with himself. If this didn't pan out he'd just have to wait until the sniper got Benotti and see if he left any clues. The thought that Benotti might bite the dust didn't bother him one iota. He would much prefer the law do the job but what real difference did it make? It would be a week at least before they heard something from the Department of Defense so all they could do was wait. He turned to some of the other matters requiring his attention. "I'm not too sure," he thought, "I'd mind seeing this guy get away clean. I haven't caught him yet."

*   *   *

There was something wrong, something different. The Hunter could sense it. The old wariness was overpowering. Benotti had returned a couple of days before and it looked pretty much like business as usual. From his concealed vantage point he had watched the estate quietly and intently. Everything seemed the same but nevertheless he couldn't shake the strange feeling that somehow, something had been altered. When he arrived back at his campsite that evening he considered his next move. Should he call it all off? No! But there was something subtly different and he had to figure it out. The next day he would pull back and check from a different perspective.

The following morning he sat back in a different vantage point—not as good as his primary but he could still see much of the estate. As usual, about 9 A.M., Benotti left for the city. He had added a convoy the past few days. There was a car with a couple of people which went in front as a guide. This didn't bother him. In fact, it was better for there was both more advance notice and he, at least, knew where the bodyguards were. As he was watching the two cars proceed down the street a movement in the corner of his eye caught his attention. He adjusted his position and his pulse quickened. There was another car paralleling the other two. Now that was strange. Was it on purpose or just chance? He would wait until evening and see if they returned.

That night the car did return. After they had parked for a while another car came up and replaced the new car he had seen. Who could they be? Not police; at least he didn't think so. But his instincts had been correct. That's how you

133

stayed alive. He followed the other car for a few more days as he had to know where they would be at all times. After a couple of days it was obvious they were providing security for Benotti. Forewarned, he could now plan for this contingency.

There was no way they could interfere in his plan. At the ambush site they had to be on a parallel route that placed them at least half a mile away. By the time they realized what had happened he would be far, far away. He knew there were four of them and they worked in two-man teams—one day shift, one night shift.

He returned to his ambush site. No one had been there; nothing on his blind had been disturbed. He had a beautiful view of the road and the curve. He would have about seven seconds to get his sights aligned. Once he fired he would pull back ten yards and then run about 150 yards to a road to his rear where his car would be parked. He was now ready.

The very next day he entered his blind early. He didn't know how long he'd have to wait but he knew he'd be here when Benotti came by—if not today, then perhaps tomorrow. He was watching the road through his telescope when he saw a car coming up the hill towards him. What luck. He drew in a deep breath and settled into his firing position, taking up the slack on the trigger. He watched the car loom up in his telescope. He picked up Benotti in the cross hairs; one, two, three, four: Click. The dry run was perfect. He couldn't miss; the next time they came this way Benotti would buy the farm.

*   *   *

The package had arrived in Wednesday's mail. Monero and Donelly had gone to work on it almost immediately. It was from the Department of Defense and had contained the service records of twelve men. As usual they split the files down the middle, each taking half to work on. And again, they finished, exchanged again and then compared notes.

Donelly had gone through four of his second set when he

picked up the one labelled *Roberts, Donald E, KIA*. His pulse quickened a little. If there was an answer it would be here. He went through the record page by page. This Roberts had been quite a honcho. He had received several decorations including the Silver Star medal and had been wounded twice before his luck had finally run out. He came across several school and unit rosters from different places before Korea. He had been assigned to an infantry unit and then transferred to a special detachment a few months before his death. Roberts attended a sniper school presented by Eighth Army Headquarters. There was a school roster and he casually read down the list. There were sixteen names in alphabetical order. He went to the R's and there was Roberts' name. He was about to flip the page and his heart stood still for a few seconds. It all came rushing back to him in a flood.

He now knew what it was about the sniper's description that had stirred his memory. It was the eyes he remembered, the sudden cold-hard slate-like look that appeared in them the last time they had met. The purpose of the killings, the method, the desire, it was all here and it was very clear. Donelly's hand was actually shaking. On the roster under K there was only one name: Knorr, Jason R.

He looked across the table. Monero was deeply engrossed in his task of screening the records. He looked surreptitiously around the squad room. No one was paying any attention to them. His heart was pounding and he could feel sweat on his forehead. His tie was too tight; he was having trouble breathing. Couldn't anyone see what was happening to him? He closed his eyes and took three or four deep breaths. "You've got to get a hold of yourself," he thought. In a couple of seconds he was calm. He went through the rest of the record. There was nothing remarkable in it.

He returned to the school roster. It seemed almost involuntary, an impulse, in which he didn't have control of his own actions. He looked around the room again, glanced over at Monero (who was still intently reading a file) and then his damp fingertips gave a little tug and the paper tore loose from the paper fastener at the top. Donelly slid the sheet halfway down the other papers, folded it in half, turned it sideways and folded it again. Still watching to see that he was unobserved he slipped the paper into his inside jacket pocket. No one had noticed anything. He put the file back with the others and quickly read the last two.

After they finished he and Monero started talking about what they had found. Nothing new or important. Monero seemed to look at him strangely a couple of times but said nothing. Donelly was nervous, but it would pass. They finally decided nothing more could be gleaned from the records and they both shortly departed to go home for the night.

That evening, as Donelly emptied his pockets and transferred his personal items to the suit he'd wear the next day, he fingered the paper in his pocket. He stared at it for at least a full minute, not comprehending what it was. How did it get in his pocket? What did it mean? He unfolded it and read it again. "My God," he thought, "what have I done? I should never have removed this from the file." His wife asked him what was wrong. He was visibly shaken, but he told her everything was okay. He just had to think something through.

He walked into his little den, sat at his desk, poured himself a stiff whiskey, and sat quietly sipping and smoking. It was circumstantial; they would have one hell of a time proving anything. *He* was sure, but could he prove it? His eyes fell on the photographs on the desk. His wife smiled back at him. In the other half of the double frame were two laughing children. His heart constricted. "If anything happened to them it would end my world," he thought. "God, the misery he must have gone through. It would probably run me off track too." He picked up the paper, held it for a few seconds and set it on fire. As he watched it burn, he thought, "He still has to be stopped." But there was no way he'd help turn him over to those animals.

22.

The next morning, Donelly walked into the office of the Chief of Detectives. He had to have a couple of days off and he'd like them starting at once. The Chief was reluctant. "Donelly, it's just a bad time. Your case load is horrendous. You also got this sniper thing. If the Commissioner heard about it he'd have my ass."

"I know Chief. I'm so close to the thing I just feel I'm losing my perspective. I can't concentrate. All I'm asking for is Friday and Saturday, I'll be back to work on Monday."

The Chief looked at him. He did look a little green around the gills. "Okay, Friday and Saturday, but you're on call if anything happens. I probably need my head examined."

Donelly thanked him and quickly left before he could change his mind. As he returned to his office he saw one of the clerks at Monero's desk. He walked over and asked her, "What are you looking for?"

The girl, completely unnerved by his sudden appearance and manner stammered, "I was asked by Captain Eddy to provide him with an update on Sergeant Monero's activities."

Donelly could see she was extremely nervous. "Is this the first time Captain Eddy has asked for that?"

"No sir. He has had me make a copy of each filed report that I've typed for Sergeant Monero. He said it was to keep him informed because you were all working on the same case."

"And what exactly were you looking for today?" asked Donelly.

"He knew you had received some military records and wanted a list of the names, but I can't find any. Sergeant Monero already sent them back."

"It's okay," replied Donelly, "I'll give you the list. Come into my office."

He gave the girl a list omitting Roberts' name. After she left he thought for a long time. Captain Eddy. It fit like a glove but could he substantiate it? Eddy had no right to the information he had been collecting, and especially the way he had been collecting it. He had been providing him with everything he thought necessary on a need-to-know basis all along. He had every intention of telling the Chief about Eddy later but he had to be careful or he'd be the one under the axe. If you were talking about superiors you moved cautiously. When Monero came in a bit later he told him he'd be off the next two days and asked him to keep tabs and brief him later.

The next morning Donelly was up at his regular time. He hadn't told his wife he had time off. He had some things he wanted to do and didn't want to be disturbed. He knew he had to be careful; everything he did from now on had to be on the quiet. He went down to Headquarters and into the basement. The old sergeant on duty thought nothing of it since Monero, Donelly, and the other two had been bouncing in and out for weeks. Donelly messed around a few minutes until he knew he was alone and no one was watching. He pulled out the Knorr file and read it over quickly, then returned it to the drawer. He had all the information he needed.

He drove out to where Knorr lived. When he arrived it was obvious that Knorr was no longer there. He talked to the new owners but they did not know where Knorr had gone. Donelly looked the place over. It was a nice home. I'll bet he was happy here. He then went to where Knorr used to work. He talked with Sanders at length but he really knew nothing. Knorr's wife was at Benson, in the hospital. He might try there. Knorr had said he wanted to be near his wife if possible. It sure was tragic what had happened. Donelly said he agreed and might check back later. Sanders said okay and if he talked with Knorr to tell him his old job was still there.

He drove over to Benson. It was out of his jurisdiction but

he was unofficial. If no one got technical he wouldn't either. He checked at the hospital and found Mary Knorr was still a patient. She would be one forever, which for her might not be too long. She was deteriorating rapidly and the doctor was concerned for her. When he asked about Jason the doctor could only give him a post office box in Benson. He hadn't seen him in months. Donelly thanked him and drove to the post office. All he could find out, unofficially, was that Jason had a post office box and it was empty. Donelly was rapidly becoming frustrated. He knew he was on the right track but the man had vanished. That night, when he returned home, he told his wife he had Saturday off and they would spend a nice day together.

*   *   *

That same evening, Jason sat in his tent listening to his portable radio. He was cleaning and oiling his weapon. He hoped it would soon be over. He had decided to move away. He would ask Irene if she wanted to go with him. It would be a new start for both of them. He wanted her to go but if she didn't want to, he'd understand. He was getting used to living here in the forest and the mountains. The solitude was overwhelming. There were a couple of park rangers not too far away, and he'd cleared his new campsite with them to allay any suspicions they might have. He had been extremely careful with his fire and they were satisfied. He had told them he would stay about a month. They seemed unconcerned about it for they had campers in the area all the time.

Each morning when he got up he was always amazed at how beautiful the dawn was. The birds would sing and he had been here long enough so that some of the bolder animals had started returning. Even on those few days when it rained it was pleasant in the hills. He would eat breakfast on his way to the city and have his dinner on his way back. The only food he had around his camp was strictly for emergencies. On occasion he'd brew a pot of coffee in the evening but for the most part he ate in the little restaurants

139

along his route. "It is so peaceful in these woods," he thought, "so far away from the noise of the city." And then he heard a twig snap outside the tent. It startled him from his reverie.

He quickly covered the weapon and cleaning equipment with his sleeping bag. It was getting dark. His camp fire was casting an eerie glow around the area. He crawled from the tent and moved quickly into the shadows away from the fire. At first he saw nothing but he knew he'd heard some-one walking. Slowly his eyes adjusted to the gloom. He avoided looking at the fire and moved a little further into the darkness of the trees. At last he picked up movement to his left and silently moved in that direction. His pulse was quick but he was inwardly calm. If someone meant to harm him they must have certainly seen him leave the tent. He moved a little more to his left, towards the shadow. Suddenly the figure bolted into the fire light, across the open space and into the woods on the far side. It was a deer. Jason almost laughed with comic relief. Once he relaxed he realized how tense he had been at the sound. He returned to the tent, finished cleaning his weapon, and returned it to its carrying case. While it was dark he put it and the cleaning equipment back in the trunk of his car, and turned in. He had another long day tomorrow, as he would for the next several days—until he got what he came for.

23.

It had been a few weeks since Marco Benotti had received his card. Nothing had happened and apparently the extra security precautions had been successful. The four extra out of state people were getting restless; this babysitting wasn't in their line of work. Damoni had whipped some of the street people back into line and everything was right with the world.

Benotti was happy. The weeks away had relieved some of the tensions that had been building up. Today he really felt great. He had a swim before breakfast and then he and his wife had temporarily reconciled their differences. She very seldom said anything about his business but she had been concerned for his health. She was a good wife, almost thirty years now they'd been together. She worried too much. Why? Hadn't he always taken care of them? They had eaten on the terrace; it was a beautiful morning. He had felt so good he told her about his talk with Marconi and retirement. She was extremely happy. A simple housewife, she preferred a smaller place that she could care for herself.

The morning was so nice he told Gino, his driver, to take his favorite route, the long way around. He didn't go this way often, preferring to save it for a treat. He liked the slow ride through the woods area and only went this way once or twice a week for he didn't want to get used to it and spoil his pleasure. Gino passed the word on the CB to the lead car that they would be using route B this morning. The bodyguards, waiting some distance away, understood and their driver cursed under his breath. He didn't like this way because there were a couple of places when Benotti's car was completely out of their sight and some distance away unless, that is, they followed him on the same road. He mentioned this to his partner but the thought was rejected. They had been told to stay out of sight.

The convoy of two cars pulled out of the estate gate at

exactly 9 A.M. and headed for the scenic route. They stopped at all traffic signs and never exceeded the speed limit. A few minutes later the cover car started down its selected route. It looked like another routine morning drive. They had been here a couple of weeks and still hadn't seen any suspicious activity. There was no conversation on the CB; all was quiet.

The Hunter couldn't believe his luck. He had expected to wait days but today would be it. He saw the lead car coming up the hill and about 100 or 150 yards back, just coming into view, the limousine. The flank car entered one of those service roads. They were actually more than a half a mile away and—being on a different street—couldn't reach the limousine for several minutes. The Hunter snuggled into his firing position as the lead car entered the killing zone. He took a breath, let a little out, and took up the slack just as the limousine entered his firing range. He picked up Benotti's head in the scope, just like the dry run. He started his count; one, two, three, four: Wham! The rifle bucked against his shoulder and resettled on the target, but he wasn't watching any longer; he was starting his backward crawl from the blind. He heard the brakes screeching but he was already running through the woods towards the car.

*   *   *

It all happened so fast. The bullet had come through the window of the rear door. It struck Benotti just below and a little behind the right eye, continued its journey and went out the rear window of the limousine. The man sitting beside Benotti was showered with bone, blood and other debris. When he screamed for Gino to stop he was almost hysterical. Gino slammed on the brakes so hard the car swerved and threw Benotti's body off the seat and partially onto the screamer's lap.

The man beside Gino was on the CB yelling for the flank car to come back. There had been an accident. They spun their car around and came roaring back to where the limousine was sitting in the middle of the road. They parked the car and after a quick look charged into the woods toward where they figured the shot had come from. They came upon the blind, the ground was still warm to the touch. They fanned out to cover more ground and moved forward. They heard another car screech to a halt behind them but continued down the gentle slope. They broke from the woods beside a hard top road that was completely empty but there was the smell of exhaust fumes still in the air. There was an estate across the road maybe a quarter of a mile away. For sure nobody could have seen anything from there. They returned to the limousine. As they approached they could hear a distant siren. They told Gino what they discovered and then quickly returned to their flank car and drove off.

*   *   *

Jason drove straight through Benson and into the mountains to where his campsite was located. He drove hurriedly but within the limits. When he arrived at the campsite he cleaned and oiled his weapon and packed it away for storage. Then he carried the container to a predetermined spot and buried it along with the ammunition loader. The remaining live ammunition and spent cartridges—along with the gun oil, rags, and other paraphernalia—he rigged for destruction. Everything was put into a metal box and weighted with rocks which he would throw into the bottomless lake where he disposed of the car.

On the drive up to the mountain he had heard the news bulletin that told him he had been successful. Benotti was dead. The police were in a blue funk; road blocks were set up in and out of the city. He wasn't concerned. He lay down on his sleeping bag to nap. He thought he might just stay here two or three days. It was so very quiet. Now that it was over he felt a serenity he hadn't felt for months. As he lay there he said a prayer of thanks for being given the time to complete his task and asked forgiveness for what he had done. At peace, he fell into a deep sleep, the sleep of the Just.

*　　　*　　　*

When Lieutenant Donelly and Sergeant Monero arrived on the scene there was complete chaos. Police, newsmen, and rubber-neckers were all over the place. Lieutenant Donelly walked over to the car. It was Benotti all right. He looked around and finally the first patrolman on the scene reported to him. The only possible witnesses they had were in the car with the victim and they hadn't seen anything. There was one man standing there that Donelly faintly recognized as being one of the bodyguards. He was spattered with drying blood and tissue. The ambulance crew had cleaned his face and hands. Donelly realized that now was a good time to talk to him. He looked as though he were still rattled from the episode.

He walked over to the man and said, "Hello, Nick. Looks like you've had a rough time."

Nick looked at him. "Lieutenant, it was terrible. The damn bullet that got Marco just missed getting me too. You gotta stop this nut."

"Could you tell me and Sergeant Monero just what you remember, from the top?" Donelly asked.

Nick nodded. "Everything went routine. We picked Marco up about 8:45 A.M., the usual time. For some reason he was really feeling good. He kept talking about how beautiful it was. I hadn't seen him so worked up for weeks. Well, after he gets in the car he said, let's take route B this morning; it's further but he felt like looking at the scenery."

Donelly interrupted him. "Let me get this straight. You didn't come this way every day?"

"No," answered Nick, "we have three routes, A, B, and C. We take a different one each day decided at random. Normally Marco reserved B for special days. We came this way maybe once a week."

"So," Donelly thought, "the sniper must have been prepared to wait at this spot until his chance came along." To Nick he said, "Go on, you came this way. . ."

Nick continued. "Well, we got on the CB and told our

144

other car we would take this route so they led out as per usual the past few weeks. We got to this point, everyone was laughing and scratching and, bang, all of a sudden Benotti was sprayed all over me. It all happened so fast. Gino slammed on the brakes and when the car swerved Marco fell on the floor. The other car came screeching back in a matter of maybe two minutes. They charged up that hillside and through the woods to a road on the other side. It's obvious that's where the shot came from."

Donelly and Monero looked to where Nick was pointing. It was a good spot. "Did they find anything?"

Nick replied. "No, but they did say the ground was still warm like the shooter had been lying there a long time, waiting."

Donelly and Monero walked up the hillside to where a patrolman was just finishing his job of roping off the area. Donelly looked around but there was nothing. He knew before he looked there would be nothing to find. After they studied the area Donelly told Monero, "this guy is good. You can tell by the dried and mashed leaves he's been here several times. Each time he gathered a layer of new leaves so the area would appear undisturbed. You have to applaud his perserverance; he was prepared to lay here every day until Benotti finally came this way. At least that's my guess of what happened. As usual he had his escape all planned and it looks like he got away clean. I still want the lab to go over the area. Also, take a look on the other side of the woods to see if we can tell where he parked his car. We need any evidence we can find in this thing. He's like a phantom."

He was absolutely sure that Knorr was his man but knowing and proving were two different items. Suppose he finally proved Roberts was Knorr. This would be no problem. If he did, where would he be? He certainly couldn't prove Roberts was the sniper even if he had him for interrogation. So far they had not turned up one shred of tangible evidence. There wasn't even enough circumstantial evidence to hold him for twenty-four hours. Until he made a mistake it was unlikely they would ever catch him. He could tell no one of his suspicions because if he were wrong he would be sentencing an innocent man to death. He knew if the Organization had a name and a person they would eliminate him without hesitation, proof or no proof. For some reason he felt Monero knew, or at least suspected, what he was thinking. If he had come to the same conclusion though he certainly wasn't announcing it either. And Donelly couldn't discuss it with him because what he was doing had to be done alone. This decision couldn't be shared.

As they walked back to the cars Donelly knew the heat would really be on but there was nothing they could do. Not one scrap of evidence had ever been collected.

*   *   *

When they returned to Headquarters the place was in turmoil. Donelly had a note to report to the Chief of Detectives. It wouldn't accomplish anything but he couldn't avoid it. He told Vince to contact the apartment superintendent and see if he could get a composite picture or artist's sketch. It was their last hope.

When he walked into the Chief's office he was on the phone listening, which was a bad sign. He indicated with a curt nod that Donelly should take the chair in front of his desk. After a couple of minutes he replaced the phone. He looked at Donelly. "Well, what have we got? That's the Mayor I was talking with. I've had a dozen calls already. One came from the Capitol. What have we got?"

Donelly looked across the desk. "Nothing, Chief. This guy is a real professional at this business. He hasn't left a clue anywhere. The slick apartment should have told us that."

"The other night," the Chief said, "I covered your ass when the Commissioner and Eddy were after you. At that time you said you were working on an angle you didn't want to talk about. That's by the board now and I want to know what it was, or is, and what you're doing with it."

146

Donelly said, with a bland look on his face, "I can tell you now. We're grasping at straws in this thing. I took a mad gamble and checked out the service records of everyone involved. Monero and I have done nothing but study the records but there is no possible connection."

The Chief looked a little skeptical. "What made you go that route?"

Donelly gave a rueful smile. "Like I said, we're grasping at straws. I figure the guy is a big game hunter or has a military background. The ordinary citizen doesn't get that proficient with a weapon."

The Chief looked at him for a few moments. "Put that way, it wasn't that far-fetched an idea. As a matter of fact I'd call it a good hunch. You never accomplished anything?"

"No, sir," answered Donelly. "We couldn't find even a coincidence in the files. We came up with twelve records and not one of them were even stationed near another."

"Well, I guess that eliminates the idea. It was still a good one." The Chief continued. "Where do you turn now?"

Donelly thought for a few moments before giving his answer. "I really don't know. The guy is a good hunter or woodsman, we could follow that up, but the problem there is that a sizeable part of the male population around here are fairly good in the woods. I'm also having Vince have the apartment manager try and give us a composite to work with though I don't expect much. You know how those composites work."

"That's good thinking," said the Chief. "Keep me informed on any progress. The politicians are driving me nuts. The Capital even offered to send in state troopers but I told them we don't need them." He then hunched forward in his chair. "Before you leave there's one more thing. The other night I detected your reluctance to speak. Why?"

Donelly's heart gave a thump and his stomach started churning. So this was it. He was sure of the Chief; they had been together for a long time. "I don't know how to say this any other way," he answered. "I feel we have a serious leak in the Department. Maybe more than a leak, maybe like a complete flood." There, he'd said it; it hung in the air between them like a dense fog.

The Chief didn't answer right away. He had that far-away look in his eyes. At last he returned and focused his attention on Donelly. He had known him for years and knew he wasn't given to rash statements. "What makes you think that?"

Donelly was ready. May as well let it all hang out.

"Someone has made copies of every report I've submitted to you. Information on this case sometimes has even reached the Organization before it's reached us."

The Chief answered almost immediately, "It's obvious from the other night you suspect someone that was in the room. Christ, that even includes me."

"No, sir, I know you too well to even consider that. The others I don't know that well. I'm not even certain; just say it's a gut instinct."

"Of the other two, do you have a preference?"

"Yes, sir." Donelly wasn't happy but he had to go through with it. "My guess is Captain Eddy."

The Chief looked dumb-struck for a few seconds. When he finally regained his composure he said, "I've known Eddy for 25 years. I've never known him to do a dishonest thing. Christ, Donelly, that's a serious charge. What leads you to consider him?"

Donelly then told him about the episode with the clerk going through his case files and her answer of why she was doing what she had done. After he finished he waited for the Chief's decision. His entire career could be riding on this.

He finally answered Donelly. "Okay. I agree with you that there may be more here than meets the eye. Keep this quiet until I get back to you. It's possible someone is copying the reports again after Eddy receives them. I'll check it out, but I want to go very slow. There's a lot at stake here."

Donelly got up and walked from the office. He was actually trembling from the strain. He could feel his shirt sticking to his back from the cold sweat. But he also felt a lot better for if he was wrong the Chief would find out and they could try another angle. In any event, it was now out of his hands.

When he walked into his office Monero was there with an artist and the apartment manager. It had to be done. He'd certainly be glad when this day was over. He sat and watched while the artist and Monero coaxed information out of the nervous manager. After an hour or so the manager was finally satisfied they had it right; the picture, he felt, was a dead ringer for Donald Roberts. Lieutenant Donelly felt a rumble in his gut but walked over to where they were working on the picture. For some reason he felt another surge of relief. The picture might be Roberts but there was no way in heaven anyone would ever think it was Jason Knorr. For a moment or two he actually felt his instinct could be wrong; maybe it wasn't Knorr after all. He told Monero to have copies made and circulate it through the Department to accompany the description they had.

*   *   *

It was only a few hours after the composite was released that Aaron Greenblatt sat holding a copy. There were three others in the room with him. Everyone was jumpy and on edge. They all realized if this guy could get Marco he could get anyone. It didn't make a guy feel any better. They had all looked at the picture and Aaron would have a few copies made to pass around. They had to get some other more important matters taken care of first. He had notified Marconi at once that Marco was dead and arrangements for the funeral were being taken care of. Marconi had been furious. He wanted no stone left unturned in tracking this sniper down. He would contact some people there to pressure the locals into action. In the meantime he wanted Aaron to handle business matters until other arrangements could be made or the present arrangement be made permanent. It was not entirely up to him; it was something that would re-

149

quire a vote at a higher level. He would get back to Aaron as soon as he could. Aaron had immediately called a conference to get his leadership established. This sort of thing you didn't allow to hang for long. Positive and immediate authority had to be established, something like, "the King is dead, long live the King."

He finally placed the photocopy on the table in front of him and looked at the others. "Gentlemen, I assume you accept my temporary authority. We have some important matters to discuss so we may as well get to it."

The others shifted uncomfortably in their chairs but said nothing. He told them he had no intention of changing anything at present. Everyone would continue to march; the only difference being he would handle two jobs until something more permanent came along. He told them of his decision with Marconi and the vote that would be taken when the higher echelon got together.

He then turned to the problem of the sniper and what they could do. They all agreed what they could do was very little but the state organization was placing a couple of investigators on the case. They would have instructions to follow up on everything until they caught up with this guy.

He wanted the word out there was a $100,000 contract on the sniper's head. Anyone providing leads to his location would be amply rewarded, but the person who actually chilled him would receive the 100 G's. This amount should surely keep the hunt alive until they, or someone else, caught up with him.

In the meantime he felt they had blown their police contact for no useful purpose and would have to develop a new one. The chance of getting another that highly placed was remote but they'd have to try. He then adjourned the meeting until after Benotti's funeral.

24.

The following day Bob Fletcher obtained a copy of the drawing and ran it in on the front page of *The News*. When Donelly found out his ulcer really went wild. If that didn't turn it from incipient to actual, nothing would. Every nut in the city would be calling in and for the next few days they would do nothing but check out phony leads. He could not imagine it serving any useful purpose.

The lab had sifted every leaf where the sniper had lain in wait and could find nothing. From the imprint on the dead leaves they confirmed his approximate size. They had also checked the secondary road with no results. It was hard top and no tire tracks were evident. A couple of detectives had inquired at the house on the opposite side of the road, but they had not seen or heard anything. It was extremely frustrating. So far the sniper had done everything perfectly. Unless he made a mistake in judgement, which Donelly felt unlikely, they would never catch him.

Jason Knorr was his man, but there was no way under the sun he would prove it. He went back over all he remembered about the man; the intensity of feeling he had noticed at their last meeting and the eyes. He would never forget him. He also remembered giving him the names of the four men who were now dead. Had he realized that day, from Knorr's intensity of purpose, that what he was telling him would result in exactly what happened? Did he actually share a part of the responsibility for the events that followed that last conversation?

He also knew something no one else did. As sure as he was sitting here he knew the killing was over. Now that his man had extracted his "eye for an eye" he would disappear. He certainly hoped he would have the presence of mind to remove himself from this part of the country. He should travel thousands of miles, in fact. Even then there was still no guarantee he'd be safe. The Organization would dig and dig. They'd stay on the case longer than the police would; of that he was also sure.

*   *   *

Aaron Greenblatt was in Benotti's old office when his secretary rang. There was someone outside that wanted to talk to him. He wouldn't tell her what it was but said it was important. He said, "Send the guy in."

When the visitor entered he was slightly surprised but shouldn't have been. It was the bartender from the supper club, and he was here trying to make points. Aaron asked him what he wanted.

The bartender reached into his jacket pocket and brought out the picture Fletcher had published. "This is not the guy I remember coming into the club."

Aaron sat like a stone. "We were never really sure the guy you saw was the sniper. If I remember he was married."

"That's right," replied the bartender, "but if he was the man, this is not a picture of him."

Aaron thought for a moment or two. What if the little weasel was right? Suppose we are looking for the wrong man? To the bartender he said. "In what way would you change the picture?"

"His face was not as full and his ears weren't that large. There's something else but I can't put my finger on it."

Aaron said, "Why do you come to me? We've met before, haven't we?"

The bartender replied. "Yes, I work in Benotti's club. I saw this guy two, maybe three times and it's not the guy I saw."

Aaron thought for several minutes before he answered. What was the best way to handle this? Finally he said to the bartender, "I want you to go to the police. Lieutenant Donelly, he's in charge of the case. Tell him what you told me. He's got the resources to get the picture changed and distributed."

The bartender left and Aaron sat deep in thought for a long time. Wouldn't it be weird if the guy was right. He didn't think so but he'd like to know how Donelly would

152

handle the information. Yes, he'd be very interested.

*   *   *

It was a short time later that Sergeant Monero came into Donelly's office. He was busy handling another call from a little old lady who was afraid to leave her house because her next-door neighbor looked just like the picture in the paper. He looked at Vince as he hung up. "That damn Fletcher, I'm going to hang him by the thumbs next time I see him. I can't get anything done today but answer this stinking telephone."

Vince grinned. It was a pain in the ass, but it made him smile because all the callers wanted to talk to the top man. "There's a guy out here says we don't have the right picture in the papers. Says he's met the sniper and knows this ain't him."

"Why bother me with every crackpot that comes in?" Donelly asked. "Run his ass off before I get mad."

Vince answered. "I don't think he's a crackpot. He acts quite normal and is intelligent. You know I wouldn't bother you unless I thought it was important." He grinned a wicked grin. "I know you hate to be torn from the telephone at a critical point such as this."

Even Donelly had to crack a smile. "Okay, get the artist and bring him in."

A few minutes later the four of them sat around while the bartender gave instruction on the drawing of a new face. As the face emerged Donelly could see a very slight resemblance to Knorr. Very slight, but it was there. It would take a person who knew exactly who he was looking for to recognize him from the picture. After the artist had departed it was time to talk to this little creep.

Donelly didn't waste any time. "So you tell me you work in Benotti's supper club tending bar? How long have you been there?"

"Four years, or almost four years," came the answer.

"You've known for months we've been looking for this guy but only now you show up. Why?"

153

"I'm not really sure he's the guy. I told Mr. Greenblatt I wasn't sure. The guy came in the bar two or three times. They told me you were looking for a loner. This guy had a good-looking broad with him once."

Bob Fletcher had come in and sat down. Normally Donelly would not have let him observe the questioning of a witness but this time it might even help.

Donelly continued without interruption. "So based on a couple of visits to a bar you decide we're looking for the wrong guy?"

"It's like I said. The first and last time he was alone, like he was casing the joint, ya know?" was the answer.

"And based on that garbage you want me to change the entire description we have out on the streets." Donelly let his anger show through a little, not too much, just enough. His act was for Fletcher. He continued talking to the bartender. "Let me tell you something, you little creep. The description we have and the composite were made by a guy who's seen our sniper almost every day. We know it was him because that's where we ran down the name and the make of the car. The picture was shown to several people in the neighborhood and they also said it was him. Now you come in here weeks after you should have and report we're looking for the wrong guy. You seen him three times; this guy's seen him dozens of times. What are you trying to feed me, buster? Are you or your people trying to run us off the trail? Is that it?"

The bartender was completely devastated by the outburst from Donelly. He twisted and squirmed in his seat. How the hell did I get into this in the first place, he thought to himself. All he could mumble was, "I thought I was doing my civic duty, I'm just sure the picture you have is wrong. Mr. Greenblatt told me I had to come forward and speak up, so I'm here."

Donelly just looked at him with contempt and said, "Thank you. We'll call you if we need you again."

The man was up and out of the room like a shot. He

154

needed a drink bad after that ordeal. He'd have one or two before going back to Greenblatt. "My God," he thought, "I'm soaking wet with sweat and shaking like a leaf. You can be sure I'll keep my mouth shut from now on. I won't even give anyone the time of day." He walked in to buy a drink and the place was full of off-duty cops. He got so nervous he could hardly get his drink down. He almost fled the place; he had to get away from the cops.

After he had left Donelly turned to Fletcher. "Man, you really done a job on me with that damn picture. Half the city is sure they've seen the guy and have to report directly to me."

Fletcher didn't answer right away. When he did it was the unexpected. "You were pretty hard on that guy that just left. Somehow I thought what he said had the ring of truth to it."

Donelly's stomach growled. He realized Fletcher was a newsman, used to questioning and evaluating stories. He had to be careful how he answered that lead. "I'm sure he thought he was the sniper. He is the one who gave Benotti the first description that eventually led us to the apartment house. We know this because they leaked it to us. They wanted us to have the information so we'd locate him and they'd deal with him. I had him make a sketch. Vince should be coming back with copies any minute. We'll run them by the other witnesses for confirmation. You want a copy to run in the paper again?" He threw the last part in just to get a reaction.

"Not on your life. I bring in another picture for page one because we're not sure the first picture was correct and my editor will have my head," answered Fletcher. "I would like to know later, though, if anyone else confirms it."

Donelly said to him, as Monero came in with the copies, "We'll check it out. You can be sure of that. If we're on the wrong trail we'll change. This is the only possible lead we have and we'll stay on it till it's exhausted."

Fletcher got up to leave. "I'll leave you two beauties to

155

your work." He looked Donelly in the eye, hesitated, then said, "You've done the right thing on this. I want you to know that." He turned and walked jauntily down the hallway.

Monero and Donelly watched him leave and as he disappeared around a corner Monero said to Donelly, "That was a strange thing for him to say. I wonder what he meant?"

Donelly answered, his face slightly averted from Monero, "I don't have the slightest notion. He's that way sometimes." Having recomposed himself he turned back to Monero. "Let's get out and check these new pictures. By now the people must be so confused that anything they see will be him. My guts tell me that we have to go with the original picture."

25.

That Friday afternoon Jason Knorr called Irene from the motel in Benson and asked her if she could get away for the weekend. He would arrange for a room at a beach motel where they could be together. "Yes," she told him. She couldn't wait to see him and she would be there the next morning. After that he made the reservation, under his own name, for two days. He went by the post office to pick up his mail, if any was there. There was only one letter without a return address, his name and address typed neatly on the envelope. He stuffed it in his pocket. He'd get around to reading it later.

*   *   *

Saturday. Irene. A tender meeting at the beach motel, lunch, swim, and sleeping the afternoon away together. It was complete bliss.

On Sunday, he spoke with her. He would never go back to the city. He told her of his wife's hospitalization and of how her condition was hopeless. He loved her but that was now finished. He once again relived the ordeal of his son's death in the shopping center. The brutality of it all made him shake with emotion.

By the time he had finished retelling the story they had both been reduced to tears. Irene knew then she would love Jason until the day she died. He cared and loved so deeply that if he only transferred a portion of that emotion to her she knew she would be richer, by far, than most other lovers.

"Live with me," Jason asked. "Be my woman. I'm sure I can make you happy." It was a lot to ask of her, he knew, but he wanted her to give up her job and come with him.

She thought it over for hours. She was in love for the first time, a really true, deep, and emotional love. She didn't want to lose him; she would have him on any terms.

They picked a city in Ohio, neither knowing why, but that's where they would go. He had enough money to make

157

a down payment on a home and get them started. He would fly out the next day and she would give her notice. In a couple of weeks they would be together for what they both knew would be the rest of their lives.

*　　　*　　　*

Jason drove into the city early the following morning. He had a couple of errands to run and he had to dispose of his car. He also wanted to check in with the airlines and get flight information. His happiness was evident to anyone he met. After his stop at the bank and his visit to the ticket office he sold his car to a dealer. He was now ready to travel.

The moustache he had been cultivating was now full. He had never had one before and he thought it made him look a little like a cavalry officer. Irene had commented on it the day before: she thought it made him look handsome and dashing. It also tickled when they kissed which she didn't mind a bit.

He gave Irene a call and told her he'd be flying out that evening. He would phone her as soon as he was settled. Immediately after hanging up he caught an airport limousine.

When he arrived at the airport he checked in at the airline counter and checked his luggage. The clerk told him it would be an hour or so before they would announce boarding. "Fine," he said and decided to grab a sandwich before the flight. They would be making several stops along the way but would only have to transfer planes once, in St. Louis. He went whistling along the concourse in search of a restaurant.

He found a restaurant to his liking and went in, finding a seat in a booth at the rear. He sat down and ordered a ham and cheese on rye with a glass of milk. That should hold him until supper. Finished, he stopped at the counter, paid his check, turned and walked back out on the concourse. Then his heart almost stopped. It took him one or two seconds to recover his wits and react.

The cause of his problem was a real shaker. Standing in the center of the concourse, looking directly at him, was the bartender from Benotti's club. For Jason it was instant

158

recognition. Sweat popped between his shoulder blades and he could feel it running down his back. He turned quickly to his right and walked rapidly away. What in the hell was he doing here; one of the last people on earth he expected to see? Had he recognized me? He wasn't sure.

*   *   *

The man watched Jason's retreating back. For that split second in which they had looked eye to eye he felt he should know him. It was only a fleeting instant in time, but there had been something familiar about him. The sandy hair? The way he moved? The eyes? That was it. He had a look he had seen somewhere before but couldn't quite place it. He shrugged his shoulders. "No matter," he thought, "I have enough problems as it is."

He walked over to the ticket counter and checked in for his flight. He couldn't completely shake the feeling he had about the stranger he'd seen. He had time. Maybe he'd remember during the flight. It was a curse of people in his line of work. You met so many people.

*   *   *

That evening Jason left for Ohio. He had a letter of recommendation from Sanders to a man he knew there. Getting a job would be no problem. In two weeks Irene would join him. Everything would work out fine. He knew he'd have to return to Benson from time to time to check on Mary; that part of his life he could never forget. Irene and Mary; Mary and now Irene. There could, of course, be no comparisons and he didn't want any. It was merely that he'd remember. As he folded his coat to put it in the overhead rack, the letter he'd picked up protruded from his inside pocket. In his excitement of the past two days he'd completely forgotten about it.

He took his seat and fastened his seat belt. The plane was taxiing into takeoff position. He opened the letter. It was brief and typewritten.

Jason

I know what you've done. I can sympathize with your motive but cannot condone your acts.

159

Neither can I turn you over to the other people. I can't prove any connection with what has happened but I want you to know that I know. Take my advice and never return to this city. It would make it extremely difficult for both of us.

Donelly

After reading the note he tore it into little bits and pieces. As soon as he could he would flush it down the airplane toilet. He had known that if someone was close to figuring it all out it would have been Donelly. He had a lot of respect for him. Jason smiled a little smile. He certainly never intended to return.

*   *   *

When Jason walked up the aisle to take his seat on the plane he hadn't noticed one of his fellow passengers looking out of the window. If the man had turned his head to the front Jason would have had immediate recognition. It was the bartender from Benotti's club who, traveling to visit his family and preoccupied by his mother's illness, hadn't noticed Jason on the plane either. Not yet, anyway. And *if* he did make the connection, *if* he did recognize the man with the jaunty moustache, what then would he do?